Bob Moats

I0567272

Mistress Murders

By Bob Moats

New Edits as of Sept 05, 2012

REV-0326141630

1

Mistress Murders

ISBN – 978-0-9960634-5-6

For information and address:
Magic 1 Productions
P.O. Box 524, Fraser MI 48026-0524
Website: http://murdernovels.com
Cover design by Bob Moats
Photo www.fotosearch.com Stock Photography

Bob Moats

Other Jim Richards series books by Bob Moats

For a preview or to purchase a book, go to
http://murdernovels.com

What a few people are saying about Murder Novels by Bob Moats

Mr. Moats, I just got your novel "Classmate Murders" and have to let you know, I read it in one evening. That is the first book I have ever done that with. That was the most enjoyable book I have ever read. I just started reading e-books, and reading again, after getting my wife a Kindle. This book was my 12th, and the best. I just got Las Vegas Showgirls to (read) tomorrow evening. I look forward to reading many of your books in this series. I have been searching for an author and books that were fun, entertaining reads. Your books are just the ticket.

Regards, A new fan, Bill from South Carolina

****

Another very nice comment submitted through my website from Micki P.:

"I recently was given a kindle for my 60th birthday. The first book I downloaded was the Classmate Murders and have now read every one of the them. Today I started on the Fatal Rejection series. Thank you for the wonderful ride with Jim and Penny and all the rest of the troop. I have laughed and giggled thru the stories, my poor family gave me the strangest looks! Now I really want a little Yorkie!! Fatal Rejection so far is another great read! I will be looking out for more of Jim Richards and since you are my #1 Author, anything of yours I can find."

Special thanks to:

To my new editor Sally Berneathy who under took the task of going through the most recent copy of this book and giving it the edits it has been needing. Hopefully now it is better. If you need a great editor for your book go to http://www.sallyberneathy.com and check her out.

Thank you for purchasing this book, I hope you enjoy it as much as I enjoyed writing them for my faithful readers. Please feel free to email me to tell me what you thought about my stories. I can be reached through http://murdernovels.com thanks again!

The Jim Richards Family of Readers is listed in the back of the book.

Mistress Murders
By Bob Moats

Chapter One

My chest was still sore from the two bullets I took at the courthouse during Ralph Flagg's sentencing. Bulletproof Kevlar vests may protect you from having a bullet rip through your body, but not from the impact. It hurts. Take my word for it. I've been hit in the chest twice now, once in Vegas and now here in Michigan. My poor little Palm Treo cell phone stopped the bullet in the Vegas desert. It wasn't a Kevlar vest, but it prevented me from dying. The two bullets from the courthouse that the Kevlar stopped are now part of a plaque on my wall, next to the plaque with the bullet and cell phone from the Vegas shooting. I expected more plaques on the wall, not because I liked to get shot, but just having them there meant I wasn't killed.

I sat in my office, devoid of clients, playing Sudoku on my Palm TX for the millionth time and wondering if this was all worth it. I had been almost killed three times, and because of my investigations the love of my life, Penny, had also come close to harm. I put the Palm down and looked at my door which still lacked the flashing lights I thought about putting around it to make it look more like Las Vegas. I was wondering how Deacon and Lynn were getting along in Vegas. I hadn't heard from them in a while. Deacon looked so cute following after Lynn when we met her while investigating the showgirl murders. Like a puppy in love. Well, more like in heat.

I was thinking about going to the computer on my desk to play Mah Jong tiles when my door opened, startling me. I half expected either Trapper or Buck, but the person who did come in was a welcome sight, a gorgeous red-head. I figured she was a left over from the now closed call girl business upstairs, that she just hadn't yet heard that the police shut it down.

"Mr., Richards?" she said in a silky smooth voice, very slightly nasal but dreamy.

"Yes, may I help you?" I replied, standing up.

"I need your services," she said.

"Please, come in. Would you like some coffee?" I asked. She said no. I continued, "Well then, tell me what it is you need exactly."

She was about thirty-something, medium height, slender, well dressed, subdued red-auburn hair and beautiful chestnut colored eyes. She went to the client chair as I pointed it out. We both sat. She crossed her slim, attractive legs. Her beautiful face had a distressed look, sad, yet she also looked somewhat irritated.

"I'm in need of having my husband watched to see what it is he does during the times he's not with me," she said.

"You want him followed to see if he is cheating on you?" I asked.

"Well, yes, I guess I do suspect him of cheating, but mostly to see what he's up to. I suspect he may be planning on divorcing me, and I want to be prepared. Do you understand?"

"Oh, yes, get the jump on him and his holdings," I said.

"Then you do understand," she said with a coy little smile.

"Quite clearly now. I'll need some information on him," I said as I handed her my rate card. "These are my fees. You decide how much you want, and I'll go from there."

She studied the card for a moment then said the full treatment would be fine, she wanted all information on him. She opened her purse, took out two hundred dollars in fifties, and handed them to me for the advance. I handed her a pad and pencil.

"Would you please write down any information about him to help me get a feel for his movements or activities? List places he goes, where he works, any habits he may have, favorite drinking hole, maybe a few friends and where I can find them. I'll also need to know where he banks, the ones you know of, and names of any lawyers he may have," I said.

She busied herself writing a book and then handed it to me. I saw his name was David Paul. I asked if she had a picture of David. She took one out of her purse and handed it to me. He was a very handsome man. I could see women tripping over themselves to get to him.

"Why do you feel David may divorce you, Mrs. Paul?" I asked.

"Please, call me Rene. Well, he's been moving little things out of the house, his personal items, books, papers, things like that. Then he took out his jewelry without saying anything. I usually don't check his drawers, but I looked the other day, and his jewelry was gone," she said.

"He's removing valuables then?" I asked.

"Yes, like he's preparing for something."

"Could he be pawning the jewelry to pay gambling debts?" I asked.

"David has never been involved with gambling. We were in Las Vegas for a week, and he never once went in the casinos to gamble. He doesn't trust games of chance. Too risky, he says."

"OK, on the subject of cheating, does he show signs of having a mistress?" I asked.

"He has changed a bit in that respect, the way he's happy all the time, not like he was a few months ago. He's different, and spending more time away from me, staying late for work, things like that." She took a hanky from her purse and dabbed her eyes.

"Mrs. Paul, you're a very beautiful woman. Why would he want to divorce you?"

"Thank you, Mr. Richards, but beauty isn't always something a man can hold onto. A healthy relationship is important, too. I thought we had one, but it seems he wants more."

"Do you think he may be planning a divorce to be with this other woman, if there is another woman?"

"I was hoping you could tell me that," she said quietly.

"Of course, I'll be checking on him as soon as possible and give you my reports," I said.

She stood and said, "Thank you, Mr. Richards. I'll be waiting to hear from you."

I gave her my business card and said to call me if anything occurred that might help. She said she would and left.

I sat back and read the pad she wrote her husband's info on. He had a busy life. He was an account executive for a major bank, and he loved sports. He was a huge Detroit Tigers fan, had season box seat tickets, never missed a game when he could attend. He drove a Cadillac CTS and owned a boat. Loved to fish and went out most weekends to Lake St. Clair. He belonged to a gym, went three times a week. When did he find time for his gorgeous wife? Shame, really, she was a knock-out. But as she said, looks aren't everything. I stared at his picture, getting his face in my head so I could identify him later. Could Davey boy be fooling around?

My door opened again, and in walked a matronly woman, probably in her late fifties, but youthful looking. She was well dressed, had money judging from her demeanor, and she was leading a dog on a leash.

"Are you the detective?" she asked with an air of snootiness.

"Last time I looked at my license, I was."

She just looked at me, scrunched up her face and said, "Are you serious?"

"I can be. What can I do for you?"

"I'm Mrs. Elizabeth Truedell. I need protection, a bodyguard if you will. Do you provide that service?"

I thought of Buck and said, "Well, Mrs. Truedell, we have in the past, yes. Is this for yourself?"

"Oh, goodness, no. This is for Mr. Bennington of Sydney," she said like I knew the guy.

"Is this Mr. Bennington able to come in so I can talk to him?" I inquired.

"No, Mr. Richards, you can't talk to him. He's my dog," she said, seeming to be annoyed.

I looked down at what I recognized as a terrier breed, acting as snooty as his master. I suddenly realized the dog had on clothes, a small jacket, making him look dorky. I told her to have a seat and tell me more.

She sat and continued. "Mr. Bennington is an Australian terrier, and he is a show dog of careful breeding and training. I need to have him watched carefully. There are persons who would like to see my Mr. Bennington not make it to the AKC dog show next week. I've had threats already. They started this week."

"How did you receive the threats?"

"By phone. A gruff voice said it would be a good idea to stay away from the show, or else," she said.

"Or else what?" I asked.

"He didn't say. He just hung up after that." The dog sat up for her as her hand went to him. She scratched his ears and patted his head. "So can you provide Mr. Bennington with protection?'

I tried not to laugh and said, "I'm sure we can. I'll talk to my associate and see what kind of schedule we can set up. I'll need more information from you." I handed her the pad and pencil and asked her to put down names, addresses and dates of the show, along with anything else I should know.

While she was doing that, I looked at the dog; he just took a crap on my carpet.

*

Chapter Two

"Buck, you feel like doing a job for me?" I asked him when he answered the phone, sounding like I woke him. This was good because he would be groggy and more likely to agree to watch a dog.

"Well, is it a good-looking babe I have to watch?" he asked, figuring I wanted protection for a client.

"Sorry, it's a male from Australia, but he has beautiful eyes and a nice shiny coat of fur," I said.

Buck was silent for a bit, and then asked what the hell I was talking about. I told him the whole story, and he laughed loud and long.

"A frigging dog? I'm going to watch a dog to see it gets to a dog show without being kidnapped or murdered?" He was still laughing.

"It's $300 a day for a week," I said.

He stopped laughing. "When do I start?"

"Come by tomorrow morning early, and I'll set you up. I told the dog's owner to go to visit a family member tonight to avoid the threat. She agreed, but said she would need to get back to her life tomorrow, back to her business. She owns a chain of dog grooming vans that travel to people's houses to do the grooming, freeing up dog owners' lives for better things. This world is getting sad," I said.

He snorted, and then laughed again, I liked Buck's laugh. It was infectious. He said he'd be in by 9 a.m. and ready to poop scoop. I smiled and said that wasn't necessary, she had assistants to clean up after the dog. He said good-bye and hung up, still laughing.

I sat back in my squeaky desk chair thinking about dogs and cheating husbands. I guess they aren't that much different. Dogs and husbands both go sniffing after any female of their own species. I pulled the pad over and looked at both the dog protection list and the cheating, possibly divorcing, husband list. I slowly worked out my plan for tomorrow in my head and called Trapper.

After a couple rings, he came on. "What do you want now, Richards?" he said, apparently checking his caller I.D. and assuming I wanted something, which I did.

"Just a tiny favor, that's all," I said.

"You mean even tinier than giving you a Kevlar jacket that saved your life, favor?" he asked sarcastically.

"OK, that was a big favor that I will probably never live down. I just need a small favor that won't take away much of your busy life of fighting crime," I said.

"What?" He was brief.

"I have a husband going to possibly divorce his wife and quietly sneaking valuables out of their house. Can you run a check on him for me?"

"Is the wife good looking?" he asked.

"A doll, red-head, great legs and thinks hubby has a mistress," I answered.

"It never fails. They all go for the other woman. The grass being greener thing. Men can be so stupid." Trapper was eating this up.

I knew he liked redheads. He claimed he was Irish, and in the past had mentioned he liked the fiery haired beauties.

"OK, if I agree to look this guy up, and if he turns out to be a hardened killer, you get to collar him, I get to console the wife." I could almost see his grin through the phone.

"I don't care, as long as she pays her bill," I said. "But I don't think he's a hardened killer. He's a bank executive and loves the Tigers, boating and fishing."

Trapper was silent for a bit, then said, "What's his name?"

"David Paul," I answered.

"Got an address?" he asked. I said yes and gave it to him.

"I know this guy, I actually know this guy. The guy with two first names. About three months ago, he was hauled in for propositioning an undercover cop posing as a hooker during a sting. He was real friendly and talked about his love for the Detroit Tigers, boating and fishing, and how he could get me a loan at five percent on a mortgage. He was really drunk at the time, so I knew he was lying about the five percent. He was out the next morning, pleaded and paid a fine. He went on his merry way, back to his life."

"Great, does he have any other skeletons in his closet?" I asked.

"Well, some blond came in after he was arrested and made his phone call. She wanted to bail him out, but he was too far gone drunk to leave, finally passed out. We told her to come back in the morning, and she did to pay his fine. She was not a red-head," Trapper offered.

"Wait a minute. You're homicide, so how did you happen to be working vice to arrest him?" I asked.

"The sting was huge, and I was on shift. They were short so I got volunteered to process the johns. Besides, I like working vice. I get to see all the nice hookers that are hauled in." He was smiling, I could tell.

"Takes you back to the Las Vegas days and the hookers in the back cells, huh, stud?" I cracked.

"You got it, sport. I had a good thing going there until Weber caught on."

"You were a pimp, weren't you?" I joked.

"I never made any money on it, just lots of favors from the other cops who indulged in my little escapades. The girls made the money. I just looked the other way and collected IOUs." He was grinning again. I could hear it in his voice.

"Well, if you could look the other way and get any further info on David Paul, I'd appreciate it," I said.

"I'll squeeze it into my busy schedule and fax it over to you. I can't get out today. The captain is hanging around the office. I think he's bored and came here to bug us. Later." He hung up.

I was debating whether to start going after David Paul or wait till I heard from Trapper's background check. I chose the latter, packed up my stuff and decided to go home early. Buck was coming in tomorrow and Trapper probably wouldn't have anything for me till tomorrow, so I decided to call it a day, go home to see what trouble Penny had stirred up for me.

I drove into the driveway of our house and parked. Penny wouldn't expect me to be an hour early, so the door wouldn't come flying open with her there to greet me. I went in and yelled that I was home. Penny came flying out of the kitchen wearing a bikini. I was a bit stunned. My mouth just hung open as she rushed to me and gave me a big hug and a sloppy kiss. I backed up and looked at her. She could really fill out a bikini for a fifty-eight year old woman.

"Are you going swimming out in the lake?" I asked.

"No, I have something better to do. You're home early, lousy day?" she asked.

"Actually it was good, slow but good. I have two new clients. I'll tell you about them later. First I want to know about the bikini."

She smiled, took my hand and led me to the back porch. In the middle of the room was a stripper pole. She finally got it.

I laughed. "Were you practicing on this thing, is that why the bikini?"

"I wanted to feel the part. We had the exotic dancer on today, and she showed a number of moves on the thing. She had me and a couple of audience members try our luck at it. She said I did real well for a beginner. After the show, a couple of the stage crew brought the thing here and set it up for me. This room was the best for it, high ceiling and lots of room. Plus, I get sunshine coming in when the shades are up." She was smiling from ear to ear.

"Did you give the crew a show?" I asked.

"No, they had better things to do than watch me flop around, but I'm practicing to get good at it."

"Well, give me a demo," I requested.

"Not hardly. I have to practice some more before I entice you with my moves." She smiled again.

"Well, let's go watch the TiVo of your show so I can see how well you did there."

She led me to the family room and sat me down, went to start up the TiVo, then plopped down on my lap and asked if I wanted a lap dance. The show came on, and we watched it, although I was having a bit of trouble concentrating on it with her on my lap in the bikini. She did quite well on the pole for her first time. I saw possibilities for interesting nights at home. The show ended, and I started running my hands around her smooth body. She giggled and jumped up, running into the hallway down to the bedrooms. I sat there until I heard her say the bikini was coming off, and then I went to help.

*

Chapter Three

Penny and I sat on the couch, snuggling, after eating a couple of subs we made with foot long Italian bread from a bakery. I told her about my day and the new cases I got, then I commented on how good she looked in and out of the bikini and said I couldn't wait till she was proficient on the pole. She said to give her a few days and she'd treat me.

"Hey, today is a special day. Take a guess," I said.

"The day before we take our son, Buck, to a topless bar?" She smiled. I had forgotten about that.

"Well, I'm afraid Buck may be tied up for a week or so with that bodyguard case we just got. We'll have to postpone it till later."

"I hate to see a grown man cry. So, what is this special day?" she asked.

"Today in 1568, The Dean of St. Paul's Cathedral perfected a way to bottle beer. We'll make a toast to him later."

"Did the church have anything to do with beer?" Penny asked.

"No, but the way I read it, most of our alcohol problems started with Monks or some religious order. I guess they wanted to keep the masses drunk and suggestible to their whims," I joked.

"I'm sure if they started serving beer in church, you'd start going."

"Yes, but only for the beer. Chips would be a nice touch, too," I said.

"You'd replace the wine and wafers with beer and chips? You're disgusting." She grinned.

We sat watching TV and toasting to the patron saint of bottled beer and then hit the sheets again, this time to sleep.

We were up and running the next morning, Penny to her show and me to solve crimes. Penny said she had a floral designer on her show and then a person from the

American Kennel Club about the dog show next week, the one in which my client was entering her terrier. I thought about Buck and how much fun he would have watching the mutt.

Penny and I kissed at the door and headed out to our respective places of employment. I got to my office and found Buck in his usual position on the lobby chair. I kicked his feet, and he shot up, ready to fight. I just backed off.

"Good morning, Jimmy!" he cheered. "I'm ready to protect and serve. Man or beast, I shall be on guard."

"Yeah, and $300 a day is a good reason to. Come on in," I said as I opened the door. Buck sat on the client chair, and I went around the desk to my squeaky chair.

Buck was dressed very smartly, black slacks, black dress shirt and a dark grey sports coat. I imagined he had his nickel plated .38 under the jacket.

I took out my notes from Mrs. Truedell and read them to Buck. He sat nodding and asked if that was all he had to do.

"Well, you have to be alert to anyone getting near or around the dog and prevent them from harming the animal. Are you prepared to lay down your life for the pooch?" I smiled.

"I got my little persuader under my jacket. I won't let anyone harm a hair on the mutt." He grinned.

"Fur, dogs have fur, not hair, but either way, I get the picture. I got something else for you," I said as I opened my desk drawer, took out a small box and handed it to Buck.

"A present for me? Jimmy, you shouldn't have." He opened the box and found it filled with business cards, printed with his name as an associate of the Jim Richards Private Investigations firm. He beamed his walrus smile and thanked me.

"You aren't licensed, but sort of covered as an employee of the firm. So do your best to make us look good." I smiled.

"You got it, boss. Now where do I start?" Buck was raring to go.

I wrote the address down and gave him a copy of the information sheet I had filled out at home that morning, explaining his duties and a few suggestions for keeping everyone happy.

"You basically have to stay in the background, but never let the dog out of your sight. Keep a sharp eye out around you for any strange activity, like men with sniper rifles." I grinned.

"Hell, man, I could just take the dog and go hole up in a motel for the week. That would be the safest bet," he said.

"Yes it would, but Mrs. Truedell has numerous functions to go to with the dog, speaking engagements for the AKC and publicity appearances for her business. You'll be busy the whole week and earn your pay," I said.

"What if I have to take a crap?"

"Take it with the dog. He crapped on my carpet yesterday. If you really have to get away for any length of time call me. I can come and fill in for you."

"OK, I'm on my way. Call the woman and tell her to expect me," he said.

"Have fun, and don't get bit by the dog." I grinned.

He made a face and left. I picked up my phone and called Trapper. I got his voice mail and left a message. Either he saw it was me and didn't answer, or he could have been in some meeting. Either way, I'd have to wait. I called Mrs. Truedell and told her Buck was on the way, that Buck would have the right to make important decisions regarding the dog's safety. He was in charge. She agreed and said she had another warning on her answering machine when she got into her home office. I said to have Buck listen to it and report to me.

After my call to her, I sat back and organized my thoughts about David Paul. My fax machine suddenly came to life and in chattered the background check on David Paul. I pulled out the paper and saw that Trapper had drawn a little hand with the middle finger up on the top page. I laughed. I read the report, and it was basically nothing. Paul was thirty-six years old, no convictions, no felonies, no parking tickets, just the arrest for propositioning the fake hooker. He was clean otherwise. According to the report, Dave was an assistant manager for a Bank of America branch that had just opened inside the Lakeside Mall, one of those storefront banks. Not exactly the bank executive that Mrs. Paul wrote on her list. Maybe he exaggerated his position to her. He had no military record, just didn't want to join, I supposed. Financially, he was comfortable, but not well off, so Mrs. Paul wouldn't get much from him in a divorce. Unless she took his boat away. His credit report was good. He could afford to buy things on the three credit cards he had. He was the All American Everyman.

I decided to go to the Lakeside Mall and get a look at his work environment, so I closed up my office and headed out. I just got in the car when my cell phone rang. It was Buck.

"Hello," I said as I was driving out.

"Jimmy, I listened to the threat on the phone. It was kinda nasty. I didn't understand the reason for not wanting a dog to be in the show, but Mrs. Truedell informed me that a winning dog can be worth a lot of money in stud fees, much like a horse. I don't buy the idea of getting rich off a dog, but, hey, it's their business, not mine. I checked the caller I.D. and, according to a buddy of mine who works for the phone company, it's a pay phone. Privately owned by a party store in Troy. I got everything settled with Mrs. Truedell. The woman is a fuss bucket, but we're good to go here." Buck took a breath and exhaled.

"What's your itinerary for the day?" I asked.

"She has to inspect her fleet of grooming vans, and then she's going to a meeting of dog owners who breed their mutts so she can get herself into the mix. She's fairly new to this whole dog show and dog breeding business, but she had money and figured she could make more with one champion dog. I feel sorry for the dog."

"Well, I'm going to check out my cheating husband, routine stuff. Keep me informed, and if you need anything, just call."

"I will, Jimmy, but I'm not promising I won't strangle Truedell if she doesn't quit calling me *my good man*," he growled.

I snickered, said I'd talk to him later and hung up. I drove out Hayes Road, up to the Mall and into the parking lot. I wandered the place for a while then asked one of the security guards where the new bank was. He told me. I went there and found a Coney Island across the way from the bank so grabbed a booth up front and watched. I could see Dave in his office. It was right in the front window. Not a good place to have an office fling unless he wanted people to watch. I ordered milk and a donut and watched. It wasn't long before a blond came in, and they became very friendly. I saw a quick kiss by his office door after he closed it. She had to be the mistress.

*

Chapter Four

Buck was just about ready to smack Mrs. Truedell for saying "Could you please keep in the background, my good man."

He bristled and said, "Look ma'am, unless you want your dog to end up as puppy chow, I would suggest you let me do my job, as you agreed." He flashed his smile and stood his ground. She looked a bit stunned and quietly said all right. She then walked away towards the ten vans she was about to inspect. Buck offered to take the dog's leash, and she finally relented, probably fearing for her life from Buck. He looked so odd, all six foot two of him, leading the small terrier along on its leash. The dog did seem to like Buck, which pleased the big man. Buck followed behind Mrs. Truedell, stopping at each van as she checked them for cleanliness and having the equipment ready. She gave each one her approval and then told her staff to go to work. Everyone spread out, going to their vans and driving off.

Mrs. Truedell told Buck to follow. She went back to her Lincoln Towne Car, and they got in, Mrs. Truedell in front and Buck in back with the dog. The driver was given the instructions as to where they would be going, and he headed out. They went to Imperial Hall on Groesbeck, and the driver pulled up to the front doors. Mrs. Truedell, Buck and the dog exited the car, went in and found the room where the local dog breeders' society was having their meeting. Everyone acknowledged Mrs. Truedell as she probably had her groomers work on most of the dogs there. She went up to sit at a table close to the front. Buck gave her the leash and hovered behind her next to a curtain, but close enough to spring into action if the need arose.

The meeting started, and the president got up and addressed the group of about 80 people and their dogs. It was a bit of pandemonium with all the different breeds wanting to get at each other. Most of the better show dogs sat on command from their masters, while the newer members' dogs were slightly unruly. Buck watched the crowd for any suspicious persons watching Mrs. Truedell or the dog.

"If we can all sit, I'll start the meeting of the Greater Detroit Dog Breeders Society." He banged his gavel and the meeting began. Buck endured the boring speeches given by various members talking about their particular dogs, and then Mrs. Truedell got up. Buck thought she did a pretty good job speaking. She didn't sound as snooty as she acted before the meeting. Everyone had a chance to talk, and a guest speaker came and talked about dog diseases and their prevention. Then the meeting ended with snacks and light conversation.

Back in the Towne Car, Mrs. Truedell asked Buck if he had found it interesting. He said it was like having teeth pulled. She actually laughed out loud.

~~*~~

Mistress Murders

David Paul and his blond friend finally left the bank and came across the way to the Coney Island. I was hoping they'd sit next to my booth, but they went about as far back as they could get and snuggled up in a booth. I took out my new Treo cell phone and carefully snapped a couple of pictures of them. The waitress came by for the fourth time asking if I needed anything more. I figured she wanted me to vacate the booth for someone ordering a bit more than I had. I was getting slightly hungrier than a donut could fill, so I ordered a Gyro. The lovebirds would probably be there for a while, so I enjoyed my food. After about forty-five minutes, they kissed then went back to the bank where the blond went off down the mall, and he went back to work. I finished my Gyro and paid my bill, leaving a rather large tip to keep the waitress happy for my camping out. I followed the blond as she browsed a few stores and then went out to her car. I followed carefully and walked past her, noting the license plate number.

She drove away, and I circled back to the bank and sat on a bench in the mall to watch Dave do his business for a while. The bank closed before the mall, so I followed him out to his car, the Cadillac CTS Rene told me he had. From a short distance, I watched him drive out. My car was on the other side of the mall, so I wouldn't be able to follow him, but I now knew what color car he had and had been close enough to get the plate numbers. I walked back through the mall to my car and headed to where the Pauls lived in Sterling Heights. I found the location of their house from the map program on my Palm TX and set the GPS to guide me. I got to the house and saw his car in the drive. He wasn't meeting up with his side dish. I saw Rene Paul come out of the house, go to a yellow Prius parked next to the Cadillac, get in, and drive away. About ten minutes later he came out and drove off. I followed as close as possible without being seen. Traffic was miserable on Van Dyke heading south, so I had to pay close attention to keep him in sight.

He went over to 13 Mile Road and Mound Road and turned into the parking lot of a restaurant bar called The Gazebo. I pulled in just as he was going inside. I put on a different jacket than the one I had worn at the mall and went in. It was dark but I could see him sitting in a booth along the wall by the windows. I sat at the bar where I could still see him. I ordered a Pepsi even though I would have liked a beer, but not while driving. He ordered a drink then sat looking bored until a shapely brunette came in and joined him. He got up to greet her. They kissed a bit friendlier than just friends and sat next to each other facing me. That enabled me to easily take a few more pictures with my cell phone. Well, this was a turn of events, a new woman. He was cheating on his mistress and cheating on his wife. He was a dog.

They sat for a while, finished their drinks, then got up and went out. I followed and got to my car just as they drove off, both in his car. They drove out 13 Mile to just past John R Road and into a motel. I knew what they had planned. I pulled onto the side of the road, brought my Fuji camera up and snapped a couple of pictures of him going into the office, then a couple more as he came out and the two of them went to a room on the front of the building. I was going to have a good amount of info to tell Rene. I couldn't imagine him planning a divorce when he was the one being unfaithful. She could hit him for everything with this.

Mistress Murders

I thought that this could be a long wait, so I decided I had enough ammo to start with even though I still wanted to find out what he was up to by taking things from his home. I started the car and drove up to 14 Mile Road and out to Jefferson. It was about 4:30 so I decided to head back home. Not much else to do.

I got to the house and Penny was in the front yard planting flowers along the porch. I remembered she had a floral person on her show today. I could just about tell what Penny was going to be into when I got home by her guests which kind of took the surprise out of coming home. Well, she always did seem to surprise me anyway.

"I think those look very nice." Commenting on the bright yellow flowers that she had along the path. I had no idea what kind of flowers they were. They just looked nice.

"Thanks, sweetie. I had the desire to beautify the house, and I got a lot of good tips from my guest today. I have the TiVo set up so we can watch it." She smiled with pride at her accomplishments in gardening. She said she was done for the day, so we went in to watch her show. I learned a bit more about the AKC dog show from her second guest. Now I knew what Buck would be going through. Afterwards we ate a light dinner of pizza rolls and fries that we nuked in the microwave. We sat on the couch and I told her of my adventures with David Paul and his harem. She looked disgusted and said some men should be neutered. I agreed and kissed her on the cheek.

"Are you fooling around?" She popped that at me.

"I'd be a fool to," I replied. "Besides, you're more than I need."

"Better remember that, sweetie, or else." She had an evil little smile on her face.

We watched TV, had our beer and chips and snuggled. We were really disgusting for an old couple.

We had just gone to bed when my cell phone rang. I answered it and heard a woman crying.

"Hello, who's this?"

"Mr. Richards, it's Rene Paul. Sorry to call you so late, but I just got a call from the police. David was arrested for murdering a woman in a motel."

Chapter Five

I asked where he was being held. She said at the Madison Heights police station. I said there probably wasn't much we could do tonight, so I'd pick her up early in the morning and we could go there to see what happened. She agreed and said she'd wait for my call then hung up. She didn't sound really anxious to go help her hubby. Could she be happy he was in this fix? I'd find out more in the morning. It was too late to call Trapper to see if he could get a heads up on what happened after I left the motel. I wondered if I would have seen something had I

31

stayed. Something to think about on my future cases, not to be in a rush.

I think I finally got to sleep around 4 a.m. and was up by 6. I got ready and dressed, then Penny and I had a light breakfast. Around 7:30 I called Trapper. He came on sounding a bit groggy himself and asked what I wanted now. I told him about following David Paul and my discoveries and about his wife calling with the info of his supposedly killing the woman in the motel. He knew what I was going to ask.

"I have an old buddy in Madison Heights. I'll call him and get his take on it." He hung up.

Ever the brief one was Trapper. I called Rene Paul and said I was waiting to hear from a friend in the local police about the circumstances of last night and would call her back. She said she wasn't going anywhere till I called. Penny was getting ready to go out the door and stopped, looking at me kind of weird.

"What's the matter?" I asked.

"I have a ghost whisperer on my show today and a psychic. I'm not sure I want to go in to work." She didn't look happy.

I knew she didn't like ghost stories or spooky movies, so I understood. "Why did you book them?"

"There's a convention of spiritualists and mediums going on at the Rock Showplace, and my producer thought it would be nice to have them talk about it. I don't particularly think it's nice to talk to the dead. Once they're gone, they should stay gone."

"Penny, as a magician with friends who did mentalism for entertainment, we talked a lot about how these psychics are 99% fakes. Don't let it bother you. Unless you personally have seen a ghost, then there aren't any," I said, hoping to ease her mind.

She just frowned and said good-bye. She went off to her car, and I wondered if I'd come home to a séance tonight. I personally don't like psychics and mediums. I've had chances to know a few, and they were all frauds. I hoped Penny didn't start a fight with her guests about the subject.

My cell rang. The caller I.D. said it was Trapper. "Hey, Chief. What's the word?"

"Well, they say your client's husband was a bad boy. He spent the evening in the motel room with the brunette you told me about, and around midnight the manager got a call from Paul's neighbor about screaming in the next room. He went there and banged on the door, but no one answered. He opened it with his pass key and found the woman in bed, bleeding all over the place. The man was nowhere to be seen, so the manager called the police. They came and finally found the man in his car passed out. He had blood on his clothes and a knife in his hand. They took him in to be examined. He was still passed out. Reminds me of the time he was hauled in here. The boy can't hold his booze. Oh, and my friend wants copies of the pictures you took."

"I didn't see them bring any bags of liquor in with them. Maybe he went out later and got it. They only had one drink while they were in Gazebo's. I left the motel around 4:30 so they had plenty of time up to midnight to get drunk," I said. "I'll email the pictures to you, and you can forward them to your friend. Thank him for the info."

"Will do. Now I have to get back to serious crime fighting." He hung up.

I called Rene and told her I'd be there in a half hour and would tell her what I knew. She thanked me, and I got ready to go. I drove out, picked her up, and headed to the police station. When we arrived, we were directed to the arresting officer, Detective Tom Richmond. I introduced Rene and myself. He asked me if I knew Will Trapper, and I said I did. He told me he was the one Trapper called this morning, that they were friends from way back. He took us to his desk. I let Rene have the chair, and he filled us in on what they had so far.

He asked me about my involvement, and I asked Rene if I could tell him. She said that would be all right. I told him how I followed Paul the day before and the things I saw. He thought it was interesting that Paul had two women on the string. Rene was fuming by the time I finished telling that story. I could hear her mutter under her breath, son of a bitch. I gave Richmond the license plate number of the blonde's car. I told him I would send the pictures to Trapper, and he would send them to on to Richmond. He gave me his email address and said to send them directly to him. I said I would.

I asked if there were any witnesses who saw Paul go out to his car and pass out. He said, "There were no persons wandering around that time of night, just the person in the next room who heard screaming around 11:45. The

34

neighbor looked out his window and didn't see anyone outside at the time. By the time the manager called and we got there it was about 12:30. Paul could have stumbled out and got himself in the car to leave, but passed out before he could."

"Were the keys in the ignition?" I asked.

"Actually his keys were in the room. He didn't take those or his wallet and cash. He may have been so drunk he didn't pay attention to what he was doing," Richmond explained.

"When I first saw them together in that bar, I thought they looked happy together. I never would have thought he'd kill her," I said.

"Being honest, there are a few things that make me wonder about this case. Like where did he get a steak knife in a motel? Did he bring it with him? And there was a half-bottle of whisky in the room, hardly enough for them to get drunk on unless they went out to a bar just before this happened." He looked at Rene and asked, "Was your husband susceptible to alcohol, Mrs. Paul?"

She just looked stone face and said, "He could hold his liquor well, but if he drank a lot, he'd go right to sleep. He wasn't a bad drunk. Most of the time he would get happy and playful." Looking at me, she continued, "I honestly can't see David doing this. It's not like him to be evil."

"Well, we have more investigating to do. I'll keep you informed," he said, looking at me. "Any friend of Willy boy is a friend of mine." He smiled. I thought I'd have to start calling Trapper "Willy boy" now.

"Thanks, detective, I'll get those pictures to you today," I said.

"Call me Tom. I'll watch for them. Well, I don't have anything more here unless you want to go to his bail hearing. I don't think the judge will let him out due to the nature of the murder."

Rene and I thanked him, and he directed us to the court room where David was due in about 20 minutes. However, it could be an hour before they got to him. We went there and waited until he was brought in and went before the judge. The D.A. and David's attorney argued back and forth about posting bail, but the D.A. won out and David was sent back to his cell to stew. As he was being taken out he looked at Rene, waved slightly, but didn't smile. Then he was gone, and Rene and I got up and went to my car. I told Rene that I would talk to him and see what he had to say. I drove her home. She was silent the whole way there. When we arrived, I asked if she would be all right. She said she would. I left her at the door and drove back to Madison Heights to talk to Richmond again. I asked him if I could get a conference with David. He said I could watch the interrogation, but my meeting would have to wait till they finished with Paul. I said I'd appreciate it if I could observe the interrogation. He took me to the room that I was getting used to, although this time I would be in a different place. He told me they'd have him in shortly. I sat and waited. Finally the door opened and in walked another suit. I nodded to him in greeting.

"You with the D.A.'s office?" I asked.

He nodded and stood in the back of the small room. I looked at the two-way mirror just as they brought David Paul in.

*

Chapter Six

Buck slept in the guest bedroom of Mrs. Truedell's home. He insisted that the dog sleep with him. Mrs. Truedell relented and then said she hadn't slept without the dog since she got him. Early in the morning Buck took the dog out for a walk and a healthy dump on Mrs. Truedell's huge property. He was enjoying the walk in the fresh morning air when he heard a pinging noise and realized someone was shooting at him and the dog. Buck grabbed up the dog and ran for the nearest trees. He carefully looked around the tree. The only place he could see where the shots might have come from was the road along the side of the property. He heard no other noises. Judging by the lack of sound from the shots, the shooter must have had a silencer on his weapon. Mighty heavy artillery for one small dog. Buck waited a while longer, listening as a car drive off. Moving carefully he came out from behind the tree, still holding the dog, and looked in every direction but saw nothing. He went back to the house and told Mrs. Truedell what had happened, that someone was serious about this. She was in a panic and wanted to call the police, but Buck said they wouldn't do much good without evidence, plus it wasn't a human in jeopardy. She thanked Buck for protecting the dog, gave a sigh of relief and asked Buck to share breakfast, which he did.

It was four more days till the dog show, and Buck was wondering why anyone would go to such extreme measures to prevent the dog from competing. Why kill the dog? It wasn't that big a deal to stop him from entering the show. What would anyone gain from this dog not winning, and would the owner of the winning dog be the killer?

~~*~~

David Paul sat at the table with his attorney, whispering to each other. Richmond came in the room and sat across from them holding a folder. He opened it and then leaned forward, asking if David objected to the session being video recorded. David's attorney said it would be fine. Then Richmond asked if he'd been read his rights, and he said he had.

"Please state your full name for the record," Richmond asked.

"David Matthew Paul," he said.

"Mr. Paul, you were found passed out in your car last night with a knife in your hand, covered in blood from a Marsha Webster. Can you explain what happened?" Richmond said, opening the conversation.

Paul sat quietly, looked at his lawyer, then said, "I don't remember."

"Mr. Paul, you were followed yesterday by a private investigator from the time you met up with a Linda Shank at your place of employment. We got her name from her license plate that the investigator noted. The two of you ate at a Coney Island, then she left and you went home. After a few minutes, you left and went to the Gazebo bar in Warren where you met Miss Webster. You had a drink there, and then went to the Madison Inn Motel where you and the victim rented a room around 4 p.m."

The lawyer asked, "Why was my client followed by a private investigator?" David looked puzzled.

"Well, it seems Mrs. Paul hired him to find out if her husband was cheating on her. Looks like she was right, and with two women," Richmond said.

David Paul's face changed from being puzzled to full-blown rage. "What the hell, she was spying on me? The bitch couldn't keep her nose out of my business." His lawyer told him to calm down and not say anything more about it. Paul complied, but sat fuming.

Richmond continued, "The P.I. provided us with the information on the two women you met with yesterday. We got Linda Shank's name off her license plates. As to the motel incident, unfortunately the P.I. left around 4:30 and wasn't there to witness the rest of the night's activities. Too bad. Since you can't remember, we just have to assume that you committed the murder."

"I didn't kill Marsha. We were in love. I would never do that to her," David shouted. Again his lawyer told him to settle down.

Mistress Murders

"OK, you passed out in your car. Did you have that much to drink to account for passing out?" Richmond asked.

"I don't understand that part. I didn't drink enough that I would have passed out. I can't remember anything after we fell asleep in bed. The next thing I knew was waking up in a cell and being accused of murder. This is ridiculous."

"So you're saying you weren't passed out in your car due to drinking?" Richmond questioned.

"I had very little to drink. I shouldn't have passed out, let alone walked out to my car carrying a knife that I'm accused of killing Marsha with." He had conquered his anger and spoke with an air of confidence. "I also don't understand if I left the keys in the room how I got into the damn car since I always lock it."

Richmond was silent for a bit, apparently mulling that statement over. Paul had made a good point. I'd never leave a Cadillac CTS in any parking lot without locking it up, so how did he get in?

Richmond took a new tack. "OK, give me some details as to how you knew or met Marsha Webster and how long you've been seeing her."

Paul looked at his lawyer and then said, "We met at the main office of my bank. She was a systems analyst, and I was attracted to her. This was about four months ago. We started becoming closer about three months ago. The branch manager found out we were involved and sent me

40

to the stinking mall branch." He frowned and continued, "I was transferred to that new Lakeside office and demoted to an assistant manager. Not what I wanted, but you understand office politics. Don't play in their back yard."

"That must have pissed you off," Richmond said.

"Well, it didn't thrill me, but Marsha and I continued to see each other after the transfer anyway."

"OK, now who is Linda Shank, and how does she fit into all this?"

Paul smirked, looked down and spoke quietly. "She's an old girlfriend I was with years ago. She recently popped back into my life, and I was enjoying her company. We've been friendly for about a month now."

"So, you've been cheating with three different women. Isn't that a bit selfish?" Richmond grinned. The lawyer started to open his mouth, but Richmond continued quickly, "Never mind that. Let's suppose you weren't the killer. Who do you think might have wanted Marsha dead and you framed for the murder?"

"I'm not sure, but she had a boyfriend that she dropped for me. He may have been pissed enough to do something about it."

Richmond tossed David Paul a small note pad and asked him to write down anything he knew about the boyfriend. Paul did.

Richmond looked at the pad and said, "David, I have nothing more to say at the moment, but I will reserve more questions for later. I'm going to follow up on a few things." He stood and went out. A big guard came in and took David from the room. The lawyer followed.

Richmond came into my room and sat on a chair next to me, propped his feet up on another chair and grinned.

"Paul said something that caught my attention. He mentioned about going out to his car without the keys. We never told him about that when he sobered up this morning. We just told him we found him in his car, passed out. So how did he know?"

"Did his lawyer have any of the details about the arrest and circumstances? Could he have told Paul?" I asked.

"Yeah, he may have been talking to my people about it. It just struck me as interesting. I'll talk to the lawyer when he comes out. I don't want to tip Paul that he slipped up making that comment. I may need to hit him with it later." Richmond sat quietly.

"How long have you known Trapper?" I asked.

"We used to be in the same squad in Clinton Township when he was a rookie there. He just got in from Vegas, and we partnered up. The guy was insane, a real nut. We got along good, then I got a better offer for money and a promotion here. I took it, but we kept in touch." He sat smiling and chuckling to himself.

I told him how I met Will and our adventures during the Dominatrix murders. I told him about Captain Weber in Vegas and some of the crazy things Will did out there. He laughed and said these were new stories Will hadn't told him. I told him about the hookers in the back cells of Las Vegas, and Richmond said that he could believe it. He said Will had a soft spot for ladies of the evening. He and Will used to spend a bit of time on road patrol talking to the working girls. Will would look the other way for them and watch out for them, too.

I now knew Trapper liked to work both sides of the law.

*

Chapter Seven

Mrs. Truedell had Buck hold the dog while they were in the vet's office to get the dog checked for any diseases or ailments before he could be entered in the AKC dog show. Buck was holding up, despite the waiting around for every little thing Mrs. Truedell had Buck doing. He carried the dog through the various stores and businesses that she visited for the sole purpose of promoting herself and her business. Buck had to admire the woman's determination for getting ahead in life.

They were finally called into the vet's exam room and told again to wait. Buck grumbled under his breath. Mrs. Truedell smiled at the dog and gave him a little kiss on his nose. Buck had begun calling the dog Benny, much to Mrs. Truedell's dismay, but she knew it wouldn't affect the dog so she overlooked it. The vet, an attractive woman, came in. Buck estimated to be in her early fifties, about a head shorter than him, nice figure, big green eyes and jet black hair. She smiled at Buck and greeted Mrs. Truedell. Buck put the dog on the exam table and stood back, admiring the lady vet.

"Dr. Winston, this is Mr. Buck. He's Mr. Bennington's bodyguard," Mrs. Truedell said, went to a chair by the wall and sat. The vet looked surprised and asked Buck why the dog would need a bodyguard.

"There have been a number of threats against Benny to keep him from entering the dog show. I'm here to make sure nothing happens to him," Buck said.

"Well, that's different. How long have you been in the animal protection business, Mr. Buck?" the vet asked.

"Please, it's just Buck. I work for a private investigation firm, but we do bodyguard work, also. This is the first time we've protected an animal. I usually guard human bodies." He smiled.

"Well, if I ever need my body guarded, I'll definitely call you. I'm sure you could do the job well." She smiled coyly at him. "Oh, and please call me Sue. Buck, would you please take Benny by the front paws and hold him up, standing?"

Buck liked the way she called the dog Benny. She was quite good looking, and Buck was getting distracted from his duties, thinking other thoughts.

The vet examined the dog, sliding her hands over him, checking his body. Occasionally her hand would brush over Buck's hands where he held the dog. Buck was getting a bit excited by the woman and had to suppress the thoughts he was having at the moment. The vet finished and told Buck he could put the dog down. She got out a hypodermic and gave the dog a shot. Buck felt suddenly nauseous as he hated needles. She apparently noticed that because she took out a lollipop from her jacket and gave it to Buck. He grinned and said thank you.

"Sweets for the big tough bodyguard." She laughed.

Sue went to another counter, wrote on a prescription pad, and gave Buck two sheets of paper. "One is a scrip for a heartworm prevention medication for Benny, the other is for you." She gave him a sexy look and smiled. She went over to Mrs. Truedell and said the dog looked fine then took the papers Mrs. Truedell had to sign her OK for the dog show. Buck peeked at the second note. It was a phone number and the words, *call me*. He gave his biggest walrus grin, picked up Benny, and followed Mrs. Truedell out, giving Sue one of his new business cards and a wink.

~~*~~

I drove back to Rene Paul's home and knocked on the door. There was no answer. I looked in the garage door window. Her car was gone. I wondered where she could be off to. I drove over to the motel where I should have spent more time last night. If I was going to take this business seriously, I needed to pay more attention to the job. I got there and went into the office. A young looking man at the desk said hello and asked if he could help me. I showed him my I.D. and said I was investigating David Paul on behalf of his wife. He nodded and said he was on duty last night when the murder happened. I looked at his nametag. It said Mike. I asked if I could call him Mike. He said it was fine with him.

"OK, Mike, what exactly happened from the time you got the complaint till the time the cops arrived and found David Paul?" I asked.

"I got the call about 11:45 and went to the room. I banged on the door. No one answered so I used my pass key and opened the door. It wasn't a pleasant sight, all the blood. I ran down here and called the police. They came and checked around. I gave them the info from his registration which had his car listed. They went to find the car and found him, smelling of booze. I had to identify him. I said it was him, and they tried to wake him but he was pretty out of it. The CSI people examined him, and then it took three big cops to carry him to a cop car and dump him inside. They left, and then the CSI people came to do their thing in the room. When they finished, they sealed the room and everybody left."

"You must have some experience with drunks coming in to get a room for a couple hours. You know what I mean?" He nodded. "Did David Paul seem like he was drunk when he checked in?"

"Well, you're right, the drunks do have a certain look to them when they indulge too much. I didn't think Mr. Paul looked all that drunked out. He looked kind of peaceful to me, like he was on drugs. I've seen a lot of that here, too. People get drugged up, and I have to get them out of the room. I hate that. Anyways, I didn't think he was all that drunk, but I'm just a working stiff, and my opinion doesn't mean a lot."

"Mike, you just said some important things that make my investigation a lot easier," I said telling a half truth, but it made him feel important to be part of the investigation. I asked if the cops were finished with the room. He said it was still sealed and he wasn't allowed to open it up for anyone. I said, no problem, and asked if the complaining tenant was still in his room. He said yes, I asked the name and room number. He said Vera Morgan in room 204. I thanked him and went out to the stairs and up to the room. I knocked on the door. It was opened by a very obese woman. She snarled, asking what I wanted. I showed her my I.D. She squinted at it for a long time. I deduced she had bad eye sight.

"Ms. Morgan, I'm investigating the case regarding the murder in the next room. I believe you made the call about the screaming you heard last night?"

"Yeah, around 11:30 they started to argue, and then I heard screaming, sounded like someone being killed. I called the office to complain. The desk guy came up and then ran off. Cops came a little while later. I stayed in my room except when the cops questioned me. I told them the same I'm going to tell you. I saw nothing, just heard noises."

"You never looked out to see what was going on? How did you see the desk clerk run off to call the police?"

"Well, I was peeking a bit and saw him go."

I looked out over the railing at the parking lot. "Do you remember where the car of the accused murderer was parked?"

Mistress Murders

She stepped out from her room and came to the railing, looking out but squinting. "I think it was over there." She pointed to the tree-lined spaces across from the building.

"Do you wear glasses?" I asked. She looked indignant and said she didn't need glasses. I thanked her and asked if I could talk more to her later. She said that would be fine. I left her at her door and went to my car.

My cell phone rang on my way back to my office. The caller I.D. said it was Trapper. "Hey, Willy boy, what's shaking?"

He was quiet for too long before he finally growled, "Don't ever, I mean ever, call me Willy boy again if you value your family jewels."

I laughed out loud and asked what he was calling for. He said he just wanted to see how the investigation was going.

"Well, there are a few puzzling aspects to the case. Maybe you can give it a fresh outlook," I said, and told him the details of Paul and the locked car anomaly.

"Want my opinion, sounds like he's being framed. Someone didn't think out the details too well. Why would they unlock his car, put him in and take the keys back to the room? Makes no sense."

"Murdering a lover makes no sense, either," I said.

*

Chapter Eight

"Yeah, well over the years of being a cop I've seen a lot of murder between lovers. Sometimes it's the biggest reason for murder, love lost or rejected. Big killer," Trapper said.

"Well, maybe Paul and his lover were at odds. The neighbor said she heard them arguing first before the screaming. But that doesn't explain the passing out and ending up in the car without his keys. You said when he was brought into your station he was a mess from drinking. He claims they didn't drink that much last night before he fell asleep in bed. Another thing, where did he get the steak knife she was killed with? I'm sure they didn't bring it with them, and Paul doesn't remember anything. This is going to be complicated."

I was just pulling into my office parking lot when Trapper said, "Well, you're the great detective, you'll figure it out." He laughed and hung up.

I went into my office and checked the answering machine. Nothing. I sat and called Buck to see how he was doing.

Buck answered after three rings. "Doggy central."

I laughed. "How's your high profile case coming along?" I asked.

He grunted. "I'm doing my best to tolerate this woman. She can be so nice one minute and so annoying the next. If it weren't for the dog I'd strangle her, but I think the dog would miss her."

"Do you need a fill in for time off? I have an idea for relief backup for you if I can get hold of Officer Becker from Trapper's squad," I said.

"Becker is good people, one of the few I've come across that I'd trust," Buck said.

"Well, let me see what I can do to give you a day off. I'm not having a good run of luck on my case. I got a cheating husband who supposedly murdered his mistress and then was found passed out in his car and can't remember a thing."

"He's probably lying. Bad memory is a great excuse for not admitting he's the killer," Buck said.

"That has passed through my thoughts. It's a mystery for now. I'll call Becker and make him an offer. You willing to share some of that obscene money you're making?" I asked.

"To get away from Mrs. Stuck-up, I'd give him a day's pay. Go ahead and offer." Buck sounded desperate.

"I'll do that. Give me till tomorrow for an answer. Talk later, and don't murder her yet." I smiled and said good-bye. It was about 3:00 in the afternoon, and I had been a busy boy.

I called Trapper back and he answered. "What did you forget?" he asked.

"I need to talk to Becker, actually," I said.

"I'm sitting here watching him swatting flies in the squad room. It's about all he's good for. Why you want him?" he asked.

"I want to see if he would relieve Buck on his doggy protection duty for a day. Think he'd like to make $300 for a day's work?"

"Hell, I'd watch a dog for $300. Can I do it?" Trapper laughed.

"You're a high power officer of the law. I can't interrupt crime fighting to have you do a menial thing like dog sitting."

"True, I'm above that. Hold on, I'll get Becker." He dropped the phone on his desk so it blasted in my ear. I waited.

Becker came on the line, and I explained what I needed him for. He sounded excited when I told him the duty and pay. He said he had the next two days off and would be glad to help. I told him to come to my office in the morning, we would go out to Mrs. Truedell's home, and Buck would fill him in on his duties. He thanked me and asked if I wanted to speak to Trapper again. I said no, and we hung up.

I sat back in my squeaky chair and pondered the Paul case. I looked at the pad of information that Mrs. Paul had filled out for me. She listed his place of employment as a branch of Bank of America in Sterling Heights. I got organized, left my office, and drove up to that bank branch off Metro Parkway. I arrived, went in and was greeted by three different people, all asking if they could help me. Did I look that helpless? I asked the nearest person who was the person in charge. He pointed to an office and said Mr. Welkie was the senior officer of the bank. I thanked him and headed that way. I knocked at the door of his office. He jerked his head up with a surprised look. I introduced myself and showed him my I.D. He asked for a closer look. I handed him the wallet, and he studied it.

He handed it back and looked at me with an annoyed expression. "If this is about David Paul and Marsha Webster, I have given my statement to the police. You're not the police, so I guess I don't have to go through all that again."

"Does the bank want adverse publicity when it becomes known that one of its employees murdered another employee? I was hired by the Paul family to work the case and to do it quickly and quietly. I'm also helping the police with the investigation." I was stretching the truth a bit, but didn't lie.

He stared at me then sighed and asked me what I wanted to know. I asked if he could tell me a little about how he knew Paul and Webster were fooling around and why it was cause to move him out to the mall.

"I got a note from someone, I don't know who, saying that they were fooling around. He was a married man, not something we condone. I confronted him, and he got rude about it, saying it was none of my business. I didn't take that kindly. I read him the office policy I established when this branch was put under my command. It states there is to be no fraternization between employees, period, unless they were married to each other, but I would not let two married persons work together. They could work in separate branches but not in the same one. That's to prevent any criminal activities."

I wondered how a couple could commit criminal activities more than a single person, but I didn't ask.

He continued, "I told him to stop his activities with Miss Webster or be transferred. He chose the transfer. I moved him out when the new branch at the mall opened. He went gladly. That's all I told the police, that's all I can tell you."

"Did Mr. Paul seem like a violent person?" I asked.

"I was not close enough to Mr. Paul to know his disposition in regards to his emotional state." He threw out the sentence like he was a psych major.

"In other words, you don't know if he had a temper," I asked.

"No," he said and sat back. "Are you finished?" He sounded like he was getting weary of it all. I took my cue.

"Yeah, I guess you aren't much help in this regard. Sorry to interrupt your busy day." I stood and went out quickly thinking what a dick this guy was.

I left his office and almost ran into an attractive, dark-haired woman about 40ish. I apologized for the near collision. She smiled and quietly asked me to follow her. I couldn't refuse such an offer. She led me down a hallway to a door that went into a small conference room with a table and four chairs. She turned, smiled at me and asked me to sit. I did. So did she.

"My name is Sylvia. I wasn't eavesdropping on your conversation, but I could hear you from the hallway. I know more about the affair of David and Marsha than stone-face was telling you." She smiled again.

"OK, Sylvia, is this going to cost me something to find out?" I smiled back.

"No, I just want to do my duty to help Dave out. He's a good person." She gave a new smile that told me she was familiar with Dave more than just as a co-worker. I wondered if she was involved with him and if she was, why would she help knowing he was fooling around with another co-worker. Maybe she was the one who sent the mysterious note to stone-face.

"It was a bit dicey at first when they started to see each other. They kept it under wraps quite well, but then they started getting sloppy, and finally we all could see something was going on. But the kicker came when there was talk about some big time embezzlement going on. Marsha worked in the accounting department as a system analyst, working with the computers on the bank's accounts. It was rumored that money was moving around, but no one was able to prove it. Just small amounts from all the accounts, too small and too many to catch. This is not official, just word from a few people in accounting. Before the bank could do anything, stone-face stuck his nose in and moved Dave to the mall. The bank wasn't happy about it, but the deed was done, and it would have looked suspicious to move him back. Instead they just watched Marsha to see if she was up to something. Well, now it's too late to catch her. She's dead. Convenient isn't it?" She smiled again.

My mind was now busy with the new information. This would put a new wrinkle in the case.

*

Chapter Nine

Sylvia had given me a few more details on the affair between Dave Paul and Marsha Webster. Not enough to make my case easier, but it gave me a better idea of the relationship between the two. I thanked Sylvia and said I had some pressing business in order to get away from her. I sat in my car, called Richmond and gave him the info on the bank fiasco. I held back the embezzlement part because that was something I wanted to follow myself. Richmond said they were really busy with a recent rash of attacks on young women hanging around a local bar, so the Paul case was put on a back burner. The Mayor and chief of police were hot to keep the publicity down on the attacks, and he was being pressured to find that culprit. I said I didn't envy him. We said our good-byes, and I hung up.

It was about 5 p.m., and I should go and see what kind of evil Penny had in store for me. Her ghostbuster guests would most likely spook her, pardon the pun, and maybe I should be there for her. I figured David Paul would be on ice for a bit longer, and I could follow the embezzlement lead tomorrow. I drove home feeling a little apprehensive but ready to deal with whatever Penny had in store for me.

I pulled into the drive and up to the house, got out and went to the door. It didn't fly open, and I had to use my key since it was locked. I always had to tell her to lock the front door. I guess the ghosts scared her into it. I went into the living room and called her, but got no answer. I went out to the porch and found her spinning around her new stripper pole. She saw me and did a little dance over to me. I smiled from ear to ear as she spun into my arms and hugged me tightly.

"I presume you had a good day?" I asked.

"I had a great day. I debunked the spook shakers and came out pretty good. I did a little exploring on the internet about the whole cold reading and medium world and Houdini's attacks on spiritualists. I was prepared, and I conquered. I'm just doing a little steam blowing off here. I'm so glad you're home." She gave me a sexy smile and said she needed a shower. "Want to join me?" I would be crazy to turn her down. I was glad I didn't come home to her in a gypsy outfit and a séance.

We soaped each other up and scrubbed good, then toweled off and went straight to the bedroom. It was early, but she was in a mood. I didn't complain. After about an hour and a half in bed she bounced up and announced she was hungry. I laughed and followed her to the kitchen. We made a good meal and then watched TV, drank a couple beers, ate chips and went back to bed, this time to sleep. I kissed her and told her I loved her. She smiled and cuddled close.

Bob Moats

We were up early the next morning. I asked who her guest was today, and she surprised me by saying she didn't know. I said I was going to be in suspense all day. She headed off to her work, and I went to my office to meet with Becker.

I was at my office by 8:40 and found Becker sitting on the hallway chair. He immediately stood at attention. I told him to relax. We had a short briefing about what was expected, and I said we should just head out to the Truedell residence after I checked my answering machine and email.

Becker and I drove out to Mrs. Truedell's home, or I should say, Mrs. Trudell's mini-mansion. We pulled into the drive in time to see Mrs. Truedell leading Buck and Benny to her Towne Car.

Buck walked quickly ahead of Mrs. Truedell and got to the car first. He stopped just short of the back car door, his ears perked. He held up his hand towards Mrs. Truedell, and she stopped. He listened for a couple of seconds then, as if he heard something, he turned with Benny in hand, grabbed Mrs. Truedell's arm and pulled her away from the car, yelling, "Run, run, run!"

They did. Buck got Mrs. Truedell into the front door of the house, handed her Benny's leash, and said to stay right there. He carefully went back down the porch and got flat on the ground to look under the car from about 20 feet away. As this curious scenario played out, Becker and I continued up the big circular drive leading off to the right by the garages. Just as I stopped my car, an explosion lifted Truedell's car about four feet off the ground while a ball of yellow-orange flame shot out from the back.

57

Luckily, Buck was flat to the ground, but he was still being pelted with small debris, and a bumper missed his head by inches.

I pulled out my Treo cell phone and called 911, requesting they send the fire trucks out to a car fire. Becker and I jumped out of my car and ran over to Buck where he still lay on the ground. We helped him up. He shook his head and stuck his fingers in his ears, wiggling them around. I asked if he was all right. He looked at me as though he didn't hear a word I said. He yelled that his ears were ringing. Mrs. Truedell stood at her front door looking pale and terrified. Buck yelled that he had heard a mechanical noise that he recognized from his younger days when the biker gangs were at war and car bombs were an everyday occurrence.

"Where's the driver?" I asked. We all looked around and couldn't see him. I asked if he was in the car, and Buck said he didn't think so, he didn't see him as they approached the car.

Buck, Becker and I went up to Mrs. Truedell. I asked, "Your driver, do you know where he is?"

She replied, "No."

"How long has he worked for you?"

"About a month. I hired him after my last driver, Travis, left."

"Did this new driver come with references?" I asked.

"Of, course. I never hire someone without checking them first."

I asked Buck and Becker to check around to see if they could find the driver. They headed toward the garage. Mrs. Truedell and I watched the car burn.

"Why would anyone want to do this to my little dog? We could have both died in that fire," Mrs. Truedell said quietly.

"I'm not sure if this is just about your dog, ma'am. Do you have any enemies that may have wanted to harm you?" I asked.

"None that I can think of. I get along with everyone I meet," she said.

I heard Buck yell my name and I ran in the direction his voice came from. The garage door was open. I went in and found Buck and Becker kneeling at the body of the driver.

"Is he alive?" I asked.

"Yeah, just knocked out," Buck replied.

The driver started to stir. He looked up at Buck and gave a tiny scream. Becker held out his badge and told him he was safe now. The driver laid his head back on the ground and groaned.

I could hear the scream of the sirens from the fire department coming down the road. I went out the drive to watch them pull in and set out their equipment. After a half hour, they had the blaze under control. I pulled Buck aside.

"I'm thinking there is more to this than just a threat against a dog," I said.

"I was thinking the same thing. This is more than a crazy way to kill a dog. Truedell and I would have been toast if we'd sat in that car waiting for the driver who wouldn't have come. Think it's time to bring in the cops."

"Guess what, we're in Clinton Township, so who do you think I'm calling?" I grinned.

Buck didn't have to be told. Becker came up, and I told him our suspicions then pulled out my phone to call Trapper. He wasn't happy that I disturbed his late breakfast and asked me if Becker was still there. I told him he was, and Trapper said that he was putting Becker in charge to give the boy some experience. I accused him of not wanting to come out on such a menial case. I could tell he was grinning as he said, of course. He said he would swing by later to check on the progress then hung up. I looked at Becker who was watching the activities of the firemen. I called him over and told him that he was in charge of the attempted murder case, per Trapper.

Becker grinned like a teenager who just had his first kiss.

*

Chapter Ten

Becker got on his phone and called for backup and the CSI team to check the car, then went to tell the firemen that this was now a crime scene. Next he went to talk to the driver who was sitting on the porch steps holding a wet cloth to his head.

"What's your name?" Becker asked.

"Jack Edwards," he replied.

"Jack, tell me what happened up to our finding you."

"I brought out the car and parked it in front, then went back into the garage to close the door to the house. I had left it open, and Mrs. Truedell doesn't like it open. As I turned to go back out, I was hit on the head. I don't know what happened after that," he said, sounding like he was in pain.

Becker turned to Buck and asked him to relate what happened up to the explosion.

"Mrs. Truedell and I went to the car. I moved up to open the door for her since I didn't see the driver. I heard a mechanical noise, like the un-winding of a timer. I had heard that sound before. In my reckless days when one biker gang had a problem with another, they put together some homemade bombs. The timer is wound up to go off about two to five minutes from setting, and it triggers the explosives. In order to work, the person who planted the explosive would have had to know we were going to be in the car shortly." Buck didn't look happy. I'm sure he didn't like the idea of nearly going up in a ball of flame.

Since I had already explained to Becker the purpose for Buck guarding the dog, he knew what the situation was, but the attempted murder of humans was puzzling. He said to me that he believed there was more to this than just keeping the dog from entering the contest. Everyone now agreed on that.

Mrs. Truedell was very upset to think someone would want her dead. She went back into her home with the dog on its leash. We followed. She sat in the living room and quietly asked to be alone. Buck picked up the dog and handed it to her. She cuddled it and smiled. We went back out as the CSI team and two patrol cars pulled in the drive. Becker went out and took command; I thought he handled himself quite well. The extra cops cordoned off the area with crime scene tape and the CSI team went to work on the car.

Buck and I sat on the porch steps watching the whole process. About an hour later Becker came up and said the CSI had found parts of the timer, that it was a standard kitchen timer modified to set off the explosives. They would take it back to the crime lab and see what they could get off the pieces.

I asked, "Becker, are you on the cop clock now, or do I have to pay you $300 for a day's work?"

He grinned and said, "It's up to you. I'm on the cop clock now that I'm in charge. But I did have my eye on a new laptop. I was just short by $250, so I was glad for your offer." He smiled sheepishly.

I looked at Buck and said, "I'm sure you want to go home for a while and get your head together."

"Yeah, I'm really wanting to use my own shower. I think I'll head out and come back later tonight if that's OK with you," Buck said.

"Go. I can't believe you're still here. Oh, before you go, let Becker know what to do with the dog, especially the potty parts." I smiled.

Buck stood, took Becker aside and had a talk with him, then took him in to meet Mrs. Truedell. Buck came out a few minutes later, saluted me and went to his car.

Becker came out a minute or two later. "I appreciate your confidence in me. Trapper tends to regard me as a simpleton. I try to please him, but I always seem to screw up."

"Maybe you're trying too hard. Just relax and do your job. I'm sure you know what to do or you wouldn't be here, Trapper wouldn't have put you in charge of this mess," I said trying to bolster him up.

"I've been a cop for a long time, mostly street patrol; I've never done any detective work." He paused to think. "Where do I start?"

Mistress Murders

"Think about it. What would be your next step?" I asked.

He looked around at the mess in the front yard. "I'll need the results from forensics, and I'll need to know who may want to kill the woman. I guess I'd better talk to her employees. They usually want to kill their boss." He smiled, and I laughed.

"Judging by Buck's love for the woman, I'd say employees are a good place to start." Now Becker laughed.

Becker and I went back into the house and found Mrs. Truedell sitting quietly in her chair with the dog sleeping soundly on her lap. Becker went in and sat on another chair across from her.

"Mrs. Truedell, I need to have a list of all your employees, both here in the house and at your business. Can you supply me with that?" Becker asked politely.

"Yes, if you feel someone who was in my employ would want to murder me. There is a list in the top drawer of that desk. Help yourself," she said as though she was resigned to the thought that she was in danger.

Becker went to the drawer and found a folder, removed it and came back to the chair. He opened the file and sat reading for a few minutes. "Mrs. Truedell, do you have any problems, even small ones, with any of these employees?" he asked.

Mrs. Truedell sighed and said none she knew of. Becker asked if there were any persons who had been fired or quit in the last couple months that weren't on the list. She told him every person who worked for her had been with her for at least a year or more, no one had been fired or quit recently, that she had a good crew. But then she remembered that her last driver had moved to California recently, and Jack came to work for her to drive and do general maintenance around the property.

Becker looked at me and then asked Mrs. Truedell if he could talk to the household help. She reached over, pressed an intercom button on her phone and called the housekeeper. The woman came on, and Mrs. Truedell asked her to bring all the help to the library. Becker thanked her and asked where the library was. She told him, and we went there.

We found Jack, the driver, and two women, the housekeeper and a cook. Becker asked them several questions then turned the driver loose. He asked the women about the driver, and they both gave him good reviews. Becker asked them about their backgrounds, and they gave him the information. He had them write their names and addresses on a pad and thanked them for their cooperation. They left, and he stood looking a bit lost. I felt for him.

"So, I suppose you are going to talk to her business employees now?" I asked to get him on the right track. He smiled and said he was.

We went back outside, and I said I had to go back to my case of the murdered mistress. I wished him luck, said Buck should be back by 6 p.m. and I'd send Becker a check for his services for protection. He grinned and thanked me for helping him. I said if he needed anything, help or advice, just call. I gave him my card and went off to my car. I could see Becker moving back to the cops in the yard, talking.

I drove out to the Madison Heights cop shop again. I needed to talk to David Paul and see what I could get on the embezzlement slant. The desk officer told me that Tom Richmond was out on a case and would be back later. I asked where he might be, showed my I.D., and said I had some information for him. I have found in this business you have to use a lot of half-truths and sometimes outright lies. The person at the desk said Richmond was at the Covered Wagon bar checking on some recent attacks on female patrons. I thanked him and left the building.

I went to my car, took out the phone book I keep there and looked up the main branch of Bank of America. I dialed the number and asked for whoever was in charge of bank fraud and security. I was told to hold, and then a woman came on. I asked the name of the person who would be able to help with a question of bank embezzlement. She hesitated, then said the name was Frank Sitaro, but he was out of the office. I asked when he would be in as I would like to have a meeting with him. She said he'd be back around 2 p.m., and she could set an appointment with him. I said that would be fine. I looked at my watch. It was 12:45. I went to the nearest Subway and had lunch.

*

Chapter Eleven

My cell phone rang while I had a mouthful of sub sandwich. The caller ID said it was Trapper. I answered and heard loud barking. "Richards, you there?"

"Yeah, what's going on?" I asked.

"This damn dog doesn't like me. I thought about shooting it, but I'm afraid the old lady would shoot me," he said. I could tell he was smiling.

"I presume you're at the Truedell estate?"

"Yeah, I just rolled in, and Becker filled me in on his investigation. What's your take on it?"

"I observed Becker doing a fine job of investigating. Give him a chance. He'll be all right if you don't scare the crap out of him. He does fear you." I heard Trapper snicker.

"I know, I like to rattle his chain, but I'll let him alone on this one. He seems to be holding up well despite having to take the dog out for a poop. This damn mutt doesn't like me."

"Dogs are good at picking up on mean people." I laughed.

"Yeah, well, I can get meaner. So what do you think about this car bombing?" he asked.

"I no longer think it's about the dog. I think that whole thing was a smoke screen to get to Truedell. Just a cover up to make it look like she was killed as collateral damage."

He agreed with my assessment. "I'm giving Becker full rein on this one. If you and Buck could just keep an eye on him, I'd appreciate it."

I knew Trapper had a good heart, even if he wouldn't admit it.

"We'll make sure the boy doesn't come to harm. Is he nearby?"

"Yeah, want to talk to him?" I said yes, and he put Becker on. Becker said hello.

"First, what the hell is your first name?" I asked.

He laughed and said, "Barry."

I thought, Barry Becker, that's a name that must have been a problem when he was young. I suppressed a laugh and said, "OK, Barry, I had a thought. If the timer was on such a short fuse, say under five minutes like Buck said, the killer would have had to be nearby. Maybe he still is. Think about it." He thanked me, and I asked to speak to Trapper again.

He came on and said, "Yeah?"

Bob Moats

I gave him the info I got about Dave and Marsha having their office affair that resulted in his transfer. I swore him to secrecy about the embezzlement until I got more facts from the bank fraud department, which I was about to do.

"Sounds like the two were up to no good and that may have been motive for murder, either between themselves or from someone who knew what they were up to and wanted in," Trapper theorized.

"So many questions, so few answers so far," I said.

The dog started barking again and Trapper said he was getting out of there, to safer places, like a crime scene. I told him I'd talk to him later and hung up.

I finished my lunch and looked up the bank's location on my Palm TX map program then set the GPS. I drove to the bank following the voice from my Palm guiding me to the parking lot of the bank headquarters. I went into the ornate lobby. They definitely had money to burn for decorations. I told the receptionist I had an appointment with Frank Sitaro, and she directed me to the third floor office of Fraud and Security. I headed up, found Frank Sitaro's office and waited while his secretary called him. He came to a door at one side of the waiting area and invited me in. He offered me a chair and I sat. I handed him my business card.

"I guess we're sort of in the same business, Mr. Richards," he said. "We both investigate crimes. What can I do for you?"

"Well, I'm investigating David Paul and the recent murder of Marsha Webster. I'm sure you're aware of the case."

"Yes, messy thing. Sorry it happened. Anything you may know about it?" he asked.

"Well, I have heard that there were suspicions about a possible embezzlement by the two of them. You have anything on that?"

He went a little rigid when I said that. "I'm not really at liberty to discuss the possible embezzlement of funds, but may I ask how you know about it?"

"I'm a good detective." I grinned. He laughed and relaxed a bit. I continued, "It could point to motive for the murder."

"OK, fair enough. Yes, we were investigating both of them, but the idiot branch manager transferred Paul out before we got a sting set up. We did put someone in accounting to keep an eye on Webster two days ago, but that's now a moot point."

"What methods were they using to take funds?"

"Well, as best as we can figure, they were siphoning off tiny amounts of interest from each account. With thousands of accounts, that could amount to a large fortune. They would do it around the ending cycle of monthly billing, so it changed before we could see it. It would have taken a clever software program to do something this huge. It's something I don't honestly understand, but our computer people do. They inform me when it happens, and I act on it."

"So do you have any idea of how much they may have gotten already?"

"Well, my computer people said the program they used, if running for a couple months, would amount to a couple million dollars. We still aren't sure where they were sending the funds, but we're working on it. Hopefully we'll know by next week now that we've moved in on Webster's work computer," he said with a sigh of relief.

"Do you have anything positive on David Paul to link him to this?"

"No, right now it's just speculation that he had anything to do with it. We can't pin this on him, and now Webster's gone, so we just need to get the funds back and close the case. If you discover anything that may help our case, and it leads to recovering money, there would be a finder's fee in it." He smiled.

"Well, I'll have to step up my detecting, won't I?" I grinned, thanked him for his time, and went to take one of his cards. He stopped me. He wrote his cell phone number on the back of it and returned it to me.

"Just in case you find anything." He stood and walked me to the door.

I left the building, now motivated by a large fee if I could crack the case. I wasn't even sure if Mrs. Paul was going to pay me since I hadn't completed her case for her.

Mistress Murders

I was wondering what Rene Paul was up to and since I was a short distance from her home I decided to go there.

I drove to the house and found her Prius in her drive. I parked on the street since my trusty, but old, Crown Vic had an oil leak, and I didn't want to soil her drive. I went to the door just as she was coming out with a tall, handsome man. She looked surprised and sputtered a hello to me.

"I was in the area and thought I would come by and fill you in on the murder case, but if you're otherwise involved, I can come by another time," I offered. I wondered who her friend was, but I didn't ask.

"Mr. Richards, thank you, but I am in a hurry to be somewhere. Call me and I'll set some time aside for you." She looked at the man, and he walked around her, went to the Prius, and got in the passenger side. Rene looked embarrassed and said it was her lawyer, that they were discussing her pending divorce. I thought, sure.

"I apologize for coming unannounced. I'll get back to you later," I said and went to my car. They drove off, and I wondered why she would pick up her lawyer and drop him off. He couldn't just drive himself over? This was getting interesting.

It was about 3 p.m., and I drove over to Mrs. Truedell's home again. Becker was out on the front lawn looking at the car wreck, talking to another cop. He waved to me as I drove up. I got out and came around to the two men.

"I followed your suggestion, and we scouted out the property. Over on the side of the garage we found a box that probably once held the bomb. It had a shipping label on it. I'm sure not the bomber's address, but something to follow up on. I sent a car out to the address to check it."

"How's Truedell holding up?" I asked.

"She's doing okay. I'm watching her more than the dog right now. She said she would appreciate the personal protection on her life. Buck called me and said he would be here around 6:30 to take over again. He sounded rested."

"Did Trapper give you a hard time?" I asked.

"No, he was real supportivc. I liked that." He grinned. "I asked Mrs. Truedell to call all her employees to meet me at her business office in the morning to start questioning everyone."

"Good. It may be nothing, but it could break the case," I said as I stood looking at the once beautiful Lincoln Towne Car, now a mess of scorched and twisted metal. Such a shame.

*

Chapter Twelve

Becker's cell phone rang. He answered and listened for a bit, then said thanks and hung up. He said that the lab had pulled off a partial print from the timer, just enough to I.D. a felon named Edward Jackson. Wanted for prior attempts at murder with explosive devices, he was a second rate hit man. I thought for a minute and asked Becker to think about that name. What did it remind him of? He thought for a couple of seconds, and then I could see the light in his eyes glow.

"Jack Edwards, the driver. Damn, he wasn't very original. He must have planted the bomb and faked being knocked out!" Becker was just about drooling at the revelation. Becker told the other cop to follow him, and we all went into the house. Becker went to the kitchen and asked the cook where the driver bunked. She pointed to a door off the kitchen and said, through there. Becker and the other cop had their guns drawn. Becker knocked at the door. No answer. He knocked again and announced it was the police. Still no answer. Becker tried the knob and opened the door. He told the other cop he would go low. He did and went in. The room was empty.

Becker came out and asked the cook if she knew where the driver was. She said he left an hour ago, said he had something to do. She also said he took a suitcase with him. She'd thought at the time that it was odd. Becker thanked her, went into the living room and sat across from Mrs. Truedell.

"Ma'am, we now suspect the driver as the person who planted the bomb on the car and faked his attack," Becker said gently.

She stared at him. "Edwards tried to kill me? I can't believe it." She looked distressed as Becker continued.

"Can I see the application sheet you had on him?" he asked.

She put the dog on the floor, got up and went to a file cabinet in her office just off the living room. She took out a file folder, came back and handed it to Becker. He opened it and read the one sheet in it. After a minute, he handed it to me and asked my opinion. I read the brief form and told Becker I thought it was fairly standard, sounded made up. He agreed. I said it was worth checking the references but they probably were made up, too. I looked at Mrs. Truedell and asked if she had checked these references. She said she did. I handed the folder back to Becker and said it was a place to start looking for him. He agreed and stood, thanking Mrs. Truedell. We went outside again.

Becker said he was still going to interrogate the employees tomorrow, that one of them might have had something to do with it, also. I thought to myself, now he's thinking. He looked in the file again, took the car license plate number listed, gave it to the other cop, and asked him to run it from his patrol car then call in a BOLO if it came up legit.

"Why does this guy hang around for a whole month before doing the deed? What was he waiting for? Was he hired by somebody, or did he have a grudge against Truedell?" Becker pondered.

"Now you're facing the challenges detectives face in the process of finding the answer." I smiled.

"Maybe so, but this is hurting my head. As a cop, I follow the orders of the detectives and I arrest perps or chase and apprehend them. Never tried to figure out who did it," he lamented. "I can see why Trapper can be so ornery at times."

I laughed and said, "At times? He seems ornery most the time."

Becker laughed, opened the file, and looked over the references again. The other officer came back from calling the plates in and told Becker that the plate number didn't come up in the LEIN, it was a fake number. Becker frowned, looked at me and said "Well, back to investigating."

I wished him luck and said I had to get back to my case. He wished me luck, too. I drove off the property and decided to go to Paul's old bank and see what I could find out about Marsha Webster. I got there and went over to the desks of the bank service managers. One young woman greeted me and asked what kind of bank service I was interested in. I apologized and showed her my I.D., saying I was investigating David Paul and the murder of Marsha Webster. She lost that friendly bank officer smile and stared blankly at me.

"Mr. Richards, I didn't know Marsha very well. They all stayed in the back offices and kept to themselves. If you'd like I could call and have you talk to someone back there," she offered.

"That would be very kind of you," I replied.

She got on the phone and dialed a number then made a request for someone named Kim to come up. In a few moments a young man came out and was introduced to me as Kim Wong who had worked in accounting with Marsha. I asked if there was somewhere we could talk privately and he took me to the same small room where I had talked to Sylvia earlier. I wondered where she was.

"What can I do for you, Mr. Richards?" he asked.

"I'm hoping you can tell me something about Marsha Webster," I said, and got the same blank look the bank officer had given me. I wondered if that look was taught in banking school. But then he smiled.

"I knew her pretty well. She and I and the rest of accounting sometimes went out for a drink in the evening after we worked late. She was a real sweet girl, a bit ambitious, somewhat secretive and a wiz with computers. I didn't know about the affair she was having with Mr. Paul till after her murder when Fraud and Security questioned me about possible embezzlement by the two. It was all so distressing."

"Did she say anything about her private life outside of work?" I asked.

"She lived alone in an apartment off Cass and Groesbeck in Mt. Clemens. I think it was called Grandview Terrace. She once said she had a boyfriend, but they broke up. She mentioned a girlfriend who was a manager at a Walgreens on Groesbeck by 15 Mile Road. She said her name was Lucy." He squirmed in his chair, making me wonder if he had something more he wasn't saying.

"I would imagine after an evening of drinking in a bar, she might have talked a bit more about herself. Anything else you might know could help me find her killer," I said.

He looked at me as if he didn't understand something. "I thought David Paul killed her. That's what I heard."

"Mr. Paul is innocent till proven guilty, as the saying goes. I'm trying to find the actual killer, be it Paul or someone else. Did Marsha confide in you anything else that might point to her murderer?"

He hesitated, and then offered, "She did get a little tipsy one night and told me she was going to be rich soon and would then sail off with her lover. She didn't mention names so I didn't associate it with Paul, but when I asked how she was going to be rich, she held her finger to her lips and said that was a secret. She never said anything more after that."

"How long ago did this happen?"

"About three months ago. I was a bit concerned since she worked in a bank and had access to money through the system, but I let it go."

"So you had a feeling that might be what she was up to?"

Bob Moats

"Yeah, it crossed my mind. Now I hear that's what the bank thinks. Too bad she got killed over it."

"You think she was killed because of it?" I asked.

"Well, we went out a week before she was murdered, and she was real quiet most the night, not at all like her. I asked what was wrong, and she told me she was worried about the man she was seeing, that he was acting strange and she was in fear for her life. I asked why she didn't just leave him, and she said she tried but couldn't, that she was in too deep with him. Then she shut up for the rest of the night. I couldn't get anything more out of her."

"Do you have any opinions about her death?" I asked.

"Honestly, after I heard she was killed, and found out Paul was her lover—" He paused. "I think he did kill her for the money. I have to get back to work, Mr. Richards. Sorry but that's all I have for you." He stood. I thanked him and went out of the room.

Kim went off the other way, down another hallway into the building. I was standing in the hallway on my way out when Sylvia popped up from around the corner. She handed me a business card and said to call her, that she had a theory as to who might have killed Marsha.

*

Chapter Thirteen

She turned and disappeared down another hallway leaving me standing with the card in my hand. I left the bank. It was starting to rain so I went quickly to my car, drove over to Groesbeck, and into the parking lot of Walgreens. I went in and asked the girl at the register if Lucy was working. She called her on the P.A., and after a few minutes a woman came up and asked if she could help me. I showed her my I.D. and asked if there was a private place we could go to talk about Marsha Webster. She looked a little distressed but asked me to follow her. We went through the back stock room and into a small office. She closed the door and asked me to sit.

"I understand you were a friend of Marsha's?" I began the conversation.

"I was. We knew each other since high school, and she was a very dear friend. We had a lot of the same interests, especially computers, so we kind of bonded," she said as her eyes started to mist.

"I hope this isn't unpleasant for you, talking about her, but I'm trying to track down her killer."

She got a blank look. I was getting a lot of that today. Finally she said, "I thought that bastard David Paul killed her."

"Well, the police think that's what happened, but I'm just making sure it's true. I like facts more than conjecture.

80

What's your take on the relationship between Marsha and David?"

"Marsha was a kind, sweet girl and needed love. She told me she was happy with Paul, but he was married. I warned her nothing good comes out from fooling around with a married man. I know, I've been there. Didn't matter. She needed someone to love, and he provided it. At least, he provided sex. I don't know if he really loved her. Marsha only talked to me about him a little, but to me it didn't sound all that good. She said once that he seemed a little too interested in her work on the computers at the bank, and she thought maybe he was up to something. After a couple of months, her mood changed. She still seemed happy, but maybe a little too happy. She told me that she and David were going off together, that they were coming into some money, and they would be happy together elsewhere. Then she stopped seeing me as often as we usually did. She spent more time at the bank or with him." She stopped and looked at the floor for a while.

"Did you know that there's an investigation of embezzlement at her bank, that they think she was involved? Did she hint anything about that sort of thing?"

She looked back up to me and said, "I suspected something was going on. She was a geek when it came to computers. I know a bit about them myself. One time I was at her apartment and I saw on her home computer that a program was running. It had tons of numbers flying by and figures were changing rapidly in the columns. She didn't know I saw it, and I didn't ask her what program it was."

81

"Did you see anything on the columns, any headings or titles?"

"There was the Bank of America name on the top, and I would see a name like Grand Cayman go by every now and then. I refused to think she could be stealing from her bank. I know I should have said something about it, but she was a friend. What could I do? Maybe if I had said something, she might be alive today."

"Well, don't blame yourself. It probably would have happened no matter what you did or didn't do. As a friend, did you have access to her apartment, maybe a spare key for emergencies?" I hoped she had.

She paused and said, "I do have a key, as you say for emergencies. I don't know what I'll do with it now."

"Would it be a problem for you if I could take it to check out her apartment? It might help my investigation," I said.

She hesitated. I could see she was troubled. "Don't worry about it," I said. "If it's going to be a problem, I can just ask the building manager to let me in."

She picked up her purse and dug through it, came up with a key ring, took off the key and handed it to me. "I don't really want the thing anymore. Marsha's gone, and there's nothing for me there anyway." She started tearing up again. I said I had nothing more to ask and thanked her. I said I'd find my way out. I could tell she wanted to be alone.

I left the store and drove up Groesbeck to Cass where Marsha's apartment was located. I didn't know if the police had gone through her apartment yet, but even if they had, I might find something. I parked and looked for the apartment number Lucy told me. I came up to the door and didn't find any yellow police tape across it, so I was feeling lucky. The key worked, and I went in, I felt a little strange going into the home of someone who had been murdered. All her property was just sitting there alone until someone came to claim it. Kind of sad. I had a bad habit of giving inanimate objects a life of their own, and I shouldn't do that. Now I was feeling sorry for all her stuff, sitting without an owner.

I saw the computer on a desk by the side wall in the living room. It was a small apartment, one large area for living and dining with a kitchen off the dining area, then one small bedroom and a tiny bathroom. It was fine for a single person. I would have felt cramped in it.

I went over to the computer. It was turned off, of course. I hit the switch to turn it on, and it winked to life. It didn't take long to boot up and then I sat studying the desktop for icons to tell me what programs she had on the thing. I saw a file icon on the right that was labeled "Paul." I opened the folder and found it contained jpeg photos. I clicked on the first one. Her picture viewer program came up, and there was David Paul sitting in what looked like Marsha's living room. Same couch. I ran through the pictures quickly. They were all of David and Marsha, but none of the two of them together. They had no idea about the timer on a camera?

I played with the computer for about an hour and found nothing useful. Considering that Marsha had been a computer geek, this computer wasn't very sophisticated. I sat back in the desk chair and thought about calling Sitaro to fill him in on my findings just to let him know I was still following leads. However, I wasn't going to mention about the Grand Cayman angle yet, save it for my hole card.

I had my phone out and was getting ready to make that call when I heard a key enter the lock on the door. I reached for my Glock, but didn't pull it out. The door opened, and in walked Richmond. He got a shocked look on his face, put his hand to his gun, then saw it was me. I relaxed and grinned.

"What the hell are you doing in here, and how did you get in?" he asked, sounding rather annoyed.

"I'm a good detective." I didn't think he was buying that, so I told him of my recent findings and getting the key from Marsha's friend. I told him I had stopped to see him earlier, but he was off at the Covered Wagon bar. He grinned and sat on an easy chair.

"OK, I need to know everything you do, or I'll take you in for suppressing evidence even if you are Trapper's buddy." He grinned and waited.

I laughed and said I would tell him everything, but I wanted the finder's fee if I broke the embezzlement case. He looked at me strangely, and I explained the whole story from when I found out they might have been ripping off Bank of America. He asked when I had planned to tell him all that, and I said, it all just came at me today.

"I did come by to see you, but you were out chasing muggers. Have you solved that important case yet?" I smiled.

He looked embarrassed and said, "We found out it was the bar bouncer. He'd follow the women to their cars, cover his face with a mask, and molest them. Big case only because the mayor had an ownership stake in the bar so he didn't want any bad publicity about it. So you aren't buying Paul for the murder?"

"Not what I'm saying, but he had an interest in keeping Marsha alive if the money trail wasn't closed yet. Although it may have been closed, and he wanted to get rid of her and take it all. The bank dicks have no idea if he was involved, but from my questioning of Marsha's friends, it sounds like he at least knew about it, if not directly involved in it."

"Well, you saved me a lot of running around doing my job. I'll give you a twenty minute head start, and you can call me on your progress." He laughed out loud. I guess he thought he was funny. Well, actually he was.

*

Chapter Fourteen

Richmond and I sat a while going through Marsha's computer, but I could find no program that would rob a bank by pieces. He snooped around the apartment, checking the drawers and cupboards. I asked if he had a warrant, and he waved a paper at me then asked to see mine. I waved a finger at him. He had a funny laugh, sort of a snort and a wheeze. It reminded me of that dog in some cartoon that would wheeze a laugh when he did something nasty. I looked in the desk drawers under the computer and came up with travel brochures for the Cayman Islands. Looked like they'd been planning a trip. Could their bank be there, also?

Richmond came back, sat down next to me and said, "If David Paul had an offshore account in the Caymans, he would have had to go there personally to open it. They're pretty strict about who they give accounts to. As to which bank did he have an account in, there are hundreds of different banks there. He could have gone into any one of them. I'm glad you're on the case. Makes my life easier."

I thought that Richmond didn't really sound like he had his whole heart in crime fighting. Was he just skimming until retirement? I knew Trapper was a couple years from being able to retire, so Richmond must be close, also. I made a mental note to call Rene to see if David had been out of the country in the last four months.

"Well, I don't see anything here that gives me a thrill. I'll call you if I come up with anything from my investigation. You can say it's part of your investigation," I offered.

He laughed and said that he was going to have forensics come in to check the computer and the apartment now that we had our prints all over it.

I said I had another case I was working on, trying to find an attempted dog killer, and I was going to check on the progress of that case with my associates. I thought it made me sound important to have associates. I just didn't tell him those associates were a big biker and a mousy patrol cop.

We parted, and I went back to my office since it was nearby. When I got there, I had a message on my answering machine from Rene, asking me to call her. I sat in my squeaky chair and dialed her number. She answered, and I said I got her message. She apologized for rushing off earlier and said she would like to talk about her husband and my findings. I asked if she wanted to meet at her house or somewhere else. She said that we could meet at a Big Boy restaurant on 15 Mile and Moravian Road since she was going to be in that area in the next hour. I knew the place and said I'd meet her there.

She hung up, and I sat back, organizing the day in my head. I called Buck at home and asked him to keep an eye on Becker since Trapper was concerned. Buck said he liked Becker and would make sure he was all right when Becker was around the property, but he couldn't follow him outside. I said I understood and mentioned that Becker was going to talk to Truedell's employees tomorrow morning. Since Truedell just lost her driver,

Mistress Murders

Buck would probably want to drive her to her office early. He agreed, we said our good-byes and hung up.

I got myself together, drove out 15 Mile to the Big Boy, and went in. The hostess asked if I wanted a booth or the counter. I said I was expecting someone and took a booth. After about fifteen minutes, I saw Rene's yellow Prius pull in and park. She got out of her car. As she walked across the parking lot I had to admire the woman. She was good looking and had legs that showed well in her shorts. She came in. The hostess greeted her and brought her to my table. I stood as she slid in across from me.

"Sorry I just popped in on you earlier, but I was in the area," I said.

"No problem. I was just conferring with my lawyer as to proceeding with divorcing my bastard husband. Two women he had, and murdered one of them. I'm shocked." She said all this as though she were discussing a soap opera, not like a wounded wife might sound.

The waitress came over and asked if we'd like lunch. I said I just wanted a Pepsi, and Rene asked for coffee. She made notes on her pad then came back with the drinks a short time later.

I filled her in on everything I knew that I could tell her without going into the embezzlement details too deeply.

"Rene, has David been out of the country anytime in the last four months?" I asked.

"I don't know if he was out of the country, but about two months ago he said he had to attend a bank conference for three days, and he came back rather tan for a man who was supposedly in Seattle. I didn't question him about it. Maybe I should have."

I asked Rene if David had any computer experience.

"He couldn't even run our computer at home. He could get his email, but he was lost after that. I did most of the work on our computer, paying bills, things like that," she answered.

"So you took care of the phone bills. Were there any extra charges, long distance phone calls on any of your recent bills?"

"No, David had his own cell phone so he didn't often use the house phone for his calls. He never let me open his cell phone bill when it came. He always said he'd take care of it. That was fine with me, but yesterday I did take a look at one he left on his desk while he is in jail. It was filled with a lot of the same phone number that I figure was one of his whores. There were a couple of international call charges. I haven't any idea where they were to."

"Would you mind if I could get a copy of his phone bill?" I asked, wondering if he was calling his bank in sunny Cayman.

"Sure, I can run one off on the copier at home," she said.

"Do you have a scanner that you could use to fax it to me?" I inquired.

"Yes, I can do that. I'll fax it to you when I get home if that will help."

I said it would, greatly, and gave her my fax number. We finished our drinks, and she said if I would submit a bill for whatever services I had done, she'd send me a check. I said I'd fax a bill to her, and got her fax number. She joked about faxing me the money. We laughed, and I said a check in the mail would be fine. We departed the restaurant, and I watched her cross the parking lot. I sat back in my car, thinking about what she'd said and wondering if I should call Richmond or Sitaro. I decided to wait until I got the phone numbers Rene said she would fax to me.

I had had enough for one day. At sixty years old, I wasn't as eager as a thirty year old P.I. might be. I didn't want to push my limit. I decided to head back to Penny to see what she had for me tonight. She hadn't known that morning, or hadn't wanted to say, what kind of guest she had today, so tonight would be a surprise. I wouldn't mind the bikini and stripper pole again, something to suggest for later. I called Trapper to see how Becker was holding up. He answered and asked if I had solved the murder yet.

"No, I'm still working on it. Your buddy Richmond has an annoying laugh."

"Yeah, when he really gets going, he sounds like a mule in heat." Trapper laughed.

"How's your apprentice doing on the car bombing?"

"He's holding up well. I expect him in later to file his reports for the day, and he said he had some interrogations to do in the morning. Are you or Buck going to be there?"

"Buck is taking Mrs. Truedell to her office where they're going to question the employees, so Buck will keep an eye on Barry." I smiled.

"Good, I'm grooming him to take my job when I retire, so train him right."

"Will do. We'll talk more later. Right now I'm going home to see if I can get some good sex," I said, knowing Trapper lived alone.

"Yeah, and I'll go find a good hooker." He laughed and hung up.

I drove home, got to the door, and went in, bracing myself. I was suddenly attacked by six tiny yipping dogs, all nipping at my ankles. I yelled for Penny, and she came out of the kitchen carrying her cat Shadow. She saw what was going on, put the cat on the back of the couch, and came to my rescue. She picked up as many of the dogs as she could, and I reached down and grabbed the last two.

"What's going on?" I asked as the dogs squiggled and yipped in my arms.

"We had on a representative from the Michigan Humane Society today, and they had dogs and cats that were looking to be adopted."

I was afraid to ask. "So you adopted six of them?"

"Oh, God, no. I'm holding them here till the St. Clair County Animal Shelter can come and get them this evening. Since I live close, I offered to save everyone a long trip. They piled them all into my car at the studio, and I almost lost two when I got here and opened my car door. These little guys are quick." She laughed.

She pushed me back on the couch and then dumped the ones she had on me. They all started slobbering on me. I yelled for help. Penny laughed and went back into the kitchen.

*

Chapter Fifteen

The dogs had all finally settled down on the couch and were either sleeping or chewing on a couple of socks of mine that Penny had given them. I sat on the easy chair holding a teacup Yorkie that was really enjoying the belly rub I was giving it. The damn thing was cute, and it was small enough to put in my pocket. Well, a big pocket. Penny stood at the kitchen door holding Shadow and smiling at me.

"Wouldn't you like to have a cute dog like that?" she asked.

"You brought home a variety of dogs to see which one I would become attached to, didn't you?"

Her smile widened and she said, "Who, me?"

"You know I love animals, but if I had a choice I'd get a ferret. But this pup is cute," I said looking down at the nuzzling mongrel.

"What are you going to name him?" Penny threw the question at me, hoping to get an answer from me without thinking.

"Hey, I never said that little Willy Boy is going to stay with us." I smiled.

"Where did you get that name?" She laughed.

"Well, Trapper would hate me if he heard it."

"Ah, Will Trapper. I get it. So are we adopting a child?"

I let out a sigh. "Only if you agree to help take care of it."

"I'm here more than you are, I'll have to take care of it. Besides, you picked the one I like. So I think we agree," she said happily.

"OK, but I think Shadow may not like the idea."

"After the brood is gone, he'll warm up to Willy Boy. It may take time, but I'm sure of it."

"OK, but never, ever call him Willy Boy if Trapper is around. I'll explain later." I laughed.

Mistress Murders

Around 6:45 a car pulled into our driveway. The animal shelter people came and got the rest of the pack, and we told them we were keeping one. I gave them a fifty-dollar bill, knowing the shelter worked on donations. The man said he appreciated the home we were giving the dog. He and another man took the other dogs and left. I looked at the mutt in my arm and said he'd better appreciate his new home. Penny kissed me on the cheek and called me a softy.

We went back in the house, and I put the dog on the floor. Penny went in the kitchen to get dinner going. I said we didn't have any dog food, so we'd have to go out after dinner and get some doggy stuff for him. I guess I bonded with the pooch. It was following me everywhere I went in the house. Penny fixed a nice dinner of burgers and fries. Willy sat next to my chair and begged. I handed him a small piece of hamburger, and he wolfed it down. Penny yelled not to feed the dog at the table, that we needed to teach him table manners. I slipped him another piece of burger when Penny was looking away, but she turned and said she saw that.

After we cleaned up from our meal, we took Penny's car to K-Mart. I carried Willy in the crook of my arm. He was so small he could almost hide there. We got a cart and picked up a bunch of doggy toys and food. I got a nice bed that was the right size for him, but I did figure I would be sharing a bed with the mutt. The doggy bed would be good while Penny and I were at work. The cashier went nuts over Willy. She got the manager's attention, and she also went nuts over him. We managed to get out of the store with the dog before someone kidnapped him.

Back at the house we introduced the dog to his stuff and I got a board from the garage that would keep him in the kitchen while we were gone during the day. I told Penny we could leave the little kitchen TV going so he would have something to do. She looked at me like I had lost my mind then laughed.

The three of us sat on the couch and watched TV, Willy nestled between Penny and me. We had our beer and chips, and Willy had to have a chip. Penny was feeding him, and I said I hoped he didn't get a tummy ache. We all three went off to bed and while Penny and I snuggled, Willy crawled to the end of the bed and, after doing a spinning maneuver, plopped down and went to sleep.

In the quiet of the night I told Penny about my day and all the adventures I had. She was amazed I had covered so much ground for an old fart. I said it was too bad that the dog was on the bed and we couldn't bounce around like we used to. She said the dog wouldn't always be in bed with us and smiled evilly.

We cuddled, and Penny went to sleep quickly as usual while I lay there. Willy came up to me and started licking my face. I picked him up and took him out to the family room where we got on the internet. I checked various websites about Yorkies and learned a lot. While I was on the internet I checked on the Cayman Islands and learned a bit about them. There were hundreds of different banks on the island, and they all had the same basic policy about opening up an account. You had to do it in person and provide a whole lot of identification. Willy went to sleep on my lap as I explored the Cayman Islands, its culture, people, businesses and banks. I thought it would be a nice vacation to take Penny down to the islands while I did some investigating, but that would have to be decided after I got more info about David Paul and his activities.

I picked up the dog, and we went back to the bedroom where I set Willy on the foot of the bed and crawled in next to Penny. Normally she wouldn't wake if a bomb went off, but she sat up and asked if the dog was all right. I said he was, and she went back to sleep. I think I finally dozed off shortly after.

I got up early as I wanted to be at Mrs. Truedell's place of business to watch Becker interrogate the employees. Willy followed me into the bathroom to watch me shave, and then he followed me out to the kitchen to watch Penny make pancakes. I generally didn't eat breakfast so I just sat at the snack bar and watched. Willy was soon under Penny's feet, and she was talking baby talk to him. I watched them and thought about how Penny couldn't have children and she worked only about four hours a day so she was at home alone a lot. Having Willy was going to be good for her. I knew she had the cat, but cats are too independent. A dog, on the other hand, needs attention and company.

I called Willy over, put him on the couch, and snapped a couple of pictures with my cell phone to show Buck. Penny gathered her things and got ready to go to work, but not before showering Willy with love and kisses, more than I would get. She left, and I put Willy in the kitchen, making sure he had water and food. Then I spread papers all over the floor and hoped he would hit one. I put the board in front of the kitchen door. Willy looked so sad, I almost wanted to take him with me, but resisted. I did reach over and turned on the kitchen TV. I hoped he liked watching Penny's show.

I went out to my car, got in, and called Buck. He answered and said, good morning Jimmy. I said that Penny and I adopted a child last night. He made a couple of strange noises and asked what I was talking about. I told him about our new addition, and he laughed. He reminded me that in the past he had two Yorkies, something I had forgotten about him. I could picture the big man and the tiny dogs. I asked where Truedell's business was, and he gave me directions. I said that since Becker was supposed to talk to the employees that morning, I had decided to come and watch. He said Truedell was calling him to get going, so I said I'd see him there. I hung up and started the car, then headed out to the mobile doggy grooming company that Mrs. Truedell founded about four years ago.

I pulled into the parking lot and saw Becker talking to Buck and two uniformed cops. Becker was in civvies, I guess to look more the part of a detective. I parked and walked over to them. Becker greeted me and introduced me to the other cops, then said Truedell had all the employees in the cafeteria and had set up a small room to do the interrogations. He asked me if I would help by listening in. I said I would.

He looked at me and said it was time to get to it.

*

Chapter Sixteen

I went through the hallway showing Buck the pictures of Willy. He commented on how Trapper might not get a kick out of having a dog named after him. I said I thought of calling the dog George, Buck's given name. He just smiled and said he didn't think the dog would like that name. We got to the cafeteria and found about fifteen people sitting around. The two uniformed cops were stationed at the doors, and Becker was reading a paper in a folder. He asked for everyone's attention.

"As some of you may already know, Mrs. Truedell's dog's life was threatened, but we now suspect that it goes deeper than that. An attempt on Mrs. Truedell's life was made yesterday, but, thanks to the quick actions of Mr. Buck Carson, the dog's bodyguard, the attempt was foiled. The Clinton Township police are now investigating the case, and I will be asking everyone here questions in an effort to track down the person attempting this crime." Becker sounded like a pro.

I figured he heard Trapper do it so many times, he had learned well. Becker called a name, Diane Baker, and asked that person to go to the small room off the cafeteria. We followed her in.

Becker sat across from her and looked at the file containing the girl's work application. This reminded me of all the interrogations I had sat in on, except there was no two-way mirror.

Bob Moats

"Miss Baker, you worked for Mrs. Truedell for almost two years. Have you enjoyed your employment?"

The girl said yes.

"Tell me a bit about yourself and the job you perform here," Becker requested.

The girl told us all about her job and how she much enjoyed it. She loved dogs and thought Mrs. Truedell was a fair and good boss. Pretty much what they would all say, I thought.

"Do you know a person named Jack Edwards or Ed Jackson?" Becker asked, and I watched her face to see if there was a flicker of expression at the name. She said, no, and didn't show any signs of indicating she was lying. Becker asked where she was yesterday around 10 p.m., and she said she was working. Becker looked at me. I shrugged. He said he had no further questions and sent her out, requesting she send in the next person on his list. She left, and I said that his questions were good, he just needed to do the same thing repeatedly. He smiled and said he really wasn't crazy for the monotony of all this. The next person came in, and Becker went through it all again. Nothing popped on the second person, either.

About an hour and a half later, we had gone through the entire staff and Becker looked frustrated. I said one person had a strange look on his face when Becker mentioned Jack Edwards. Becker said he had noticed that, too, and he showed me the name he had written down, Bruce Hardy. It was the same guy I was talking about. Becker asked me if I would call him back in. I went to the door, called the name, and the man came back in. I told him to sit.

Mistress Murders

Becker took a sneaky stab. "Bruce, where did you first meet with Ed Jackson, also known as Jack Edwards?"

Bruce sat there and looked at Becker then at me. He was quiet for a minute then said, "I don't know the man. Should I?"

"He was Mrs. Truedell's driver until yesterday when Buck saved Mrs. Truedell from the bomb Jack planted in Mrs. Truedell's car. You never met him here at work or elsewhere?" Becker sounded a little angry hopefully in an effort to scare Bruce and not just because he was losing his patience.

"I don't know that person. I never saw Truedell's driver," he muttered.

One of the uniformed cops came over to Becker and whispered something in his ear. Becker said Bruce's full name aloud, and the cop whispered again in his ear. Becker got a big smile on his face and sat back, staring at Bruce who was beginning to get uncomfortable.

"Bruce, what's your address?" Becker asked. Bruce gave it to him. Becker looked at the uniformed cop who smiled and nodded.

Becker looked at me and said, "Jim, remember yesterday when I said that we found that box I suspected the bomb came in? Well, Forensics said the box did show trace of explosives." Becker turned his attention back to Bruce. "Well, there was a shipping label on it. I sent Officer Mayfield to check that address, and he said there was no one home. Probably because the person whose name was on the box was working here at the time." He stared at Bruce and said, "That label had your name and address on it. Careless of Jack Edwards to leave it on the box, or maybe he hoped it would be tracked back to you. You still deny knowing Jack?"

We could see the wheels turning in Bruce's head, and he started to look mad. "Damn, that bastard tried to frame me!" He sat up straight and said, "OK, I want immunity if I give you any more information on Jack or the person who hired me to set up the murder." He folded his arms across his chest and shut up.

"OK, Bruce, I'll see what we can do, but we're going to have to take you to the station for further questioning." He looked at Mayfield and asked him to read Bruce his rights then take him in. Officer Mayfield said it would be his pleasure and took Bruce out.

I was feeling happy for Becker and the luck he had over the box. Becker said he'd get hold of the D.A. and see where he could go from there with any offers for his testimony, if it panned out. Becker said he'd also run a background check on Bruce to see if he had any priors.

Becker got up, and we all went out to the cafeteria. He told everyone that they could go back to work or whatever they had to do. We went into Mrs. Truedell's office and told her and Buck what we found, then Becker said he would keep her informed. He left with the other cop, and I told Truedell and Buck I had some investigating to do on my murder case. I reminded Buck that the killer was still out there, so keep an eye on Mrs. Truedell till we caught him. Buck said he would, and Mrs. Truedell thanked me for my help. I left the office, tracked down Becker again, and gave him an envelope with a check for his day's work filling in for Buck. He thanked me, and I went out to my car.

I drove to my office to see if Rene had faxed me the phone bill. Hopefully it had what I was looking for. I got to my office, went in, found the fax in the tray, and took it to my desk. I examined the list of numbers. There were about twenty calls to one local number and sixteen to another, probably his two girlfriends. That reminded me about Linda Shanks, the blond mistress. I needed to follow up on her to see what she had on Paul, so I took the numbers and wrote them down. However, it was the long distance calls I was really interested in. I wrote down all the area codes listed on the sheet, pulled out my Palm TX and brought up the Worldmate program then pulled up the area code listings. I scanned down the list and checked each one. There were a couple of calls to Germany, which I wondered about. There were three to the Bahamas and Cayman Islands, all made in the last three weeks. I was finally finding a link.

I sat back in my squeaky chair just as my door opened and in walked Linda Shanks. Talk about coincidence. I stood and asked if I could help her. She smiled and came closer to my desk. She reached into her oversized purse and was bringing her hand back up just as the mailman walked in and dropped my mail on my desk. This distracted her long enough for me to walk around my desk and come up next to her. The mailman smiled and said good-bye. I looked down into Linda's purse and saw she had her hand on a gun. I drew my Glock and pressed it against her head, then reached down, took her hand out of the purse, and removed the gun from it. I politely asked her to be seated then took out the handcuffs I kept in my desk and secured her to the chair.

"Now that we're on a friendlier footing, what the hell did you want to do that for?" I asked as I sat at my desk, putting her gun down and holstering my gun again.

"I wasn't going to shoot you with it, just scare you," she said quietly.

"Yeah, well, my gun does shoot, and I didn't know you were just trying to scare me. I could have shot you."

She looked down as I continued, "OK, spill it, why were you trying to scare me?"

"We wanted you to back off the Paul murder case," she mumbled.

"I don't scare easily. You would have had to shoot me to get me off the case. Did you think of that?" I was yelling now, just to jar her.

She started to cry. I felt bad that I had yelled. I handed her the box of tissues and sat back.

She worked her way down to sniffling, the tears all wiped away. She looked at me with red eyes and sat back in the chair.

"I'm sorry. I'm not very good at threatening people. I told him it wouldn't work, but he said you would do it," she babbled.

"OK, slow down and explain what the hell you're talking about," I asked, making an effort to be more polite. I didn't want the water works again.

"David said if you kept snooping around, it might come out what he was up to. His whole plan would come apart, and we'd lose our reward."

"Reward? What reward?" I asked.

"The reward for recovering the money that Marsha was embezzling. David knew she was doing it, and if he could figure out where she was stashing it, we could get the finder's fee."

Now I was really baffled.

*

Chapter Seventeen

She looked at me with her reddened doe eyes and said, "About four months ago, David was chasing after Marsha because she revealed to him that she was going to be rich in a couple of months. He was curious so he asked her how, but she said she wouldn't tell yet. I came back into town after being out in Colorado, and I ran into David at the bank where he was then working. I was going for a loan on a house my family was selling, my childhood home. I wanted it. I was surprised to see him there. Years ago we were hot and heavy before he met Rene. We even talked about marriage. But then I got a great offer for employment in Boulder, Colorado, and he wouldn't move, so we parted. My great job out there finally went bust and I came back here. David and I hooked up again, but he was also seeing Marsha. He told me he had to so he could find out about the money she was embezzling from the bank. As I said, there would be a sizable finder's fee if we tracked it down." She paused.

I knew about the fee. Too bad they knew, too.

I offered, "So David was seeing Marsha to get information from her about the whereabouts of the money? There was no real affair?"

"Right. He and I fell back in love, and he wanted to get the money for us. He was fed up with his wife and wanted to be with me. Now he's in jail for the murder of Marsha, but he wouldn't do that since she was the only one who knew where the money was being transferred to. It would be stupid to kill the golden goose, as he said." She paused again.

I reached over to the phone, called Richmond, and asked where he was. He said he was back at Marsha's apartment with his CSI team. That was good, he was close by. I told him where my office was and said to get there fast. I hung up. Linda looked really frightened now. I stood and took the cuffs off her.

"I'll forget charging you for assault with a deadly weapon if you'll just sit quietly and tell Detective Richmond everything you told me," I said. "Oh, and you better hope this gun is registered."

Mistress Murders

She said it was David's. A friend of his had it, and David told him to give it to her. She was tearing up again. I put the gun in my desk drawer and said we wouldn't mention it then. I told her just to say she came in to tell me about David's innocence. I said I was sorry if the finder's fee came out, but she needed to establish David's innocence. She went quiet again.

About ten minutes later Richmond came in and asked what I had. I introduced him to Linda Shanks. He recognized the name, said he had been planning to look her up for questioning, and then he sat in the other client chair.

"Miss Shanks came in to talk to me about David Paul's affair with Marsha Webster. There's an interesting twist in the story. I told you about the suspicion of embezzlement. Well, Miss Shanks can enlighten you concerning David's involvement." I looked at Linda and told her to tell Richmond what she had just told me.

She went through it again, and when she was finished, Richmond asked why David hadn't told them this before. Linda said he wanted the finder's fee and was worried if the cops investigated it and found the money, no one would get the fee. Richmond sat for a bit then stood.

"I'll go back and question Paul again and see if we can get his facts straight. I'm still baffled by a few details in the murder. Maybe I can jog his memory now." He thanked me, and I asked if I was going to be able to talk to Paul myself. He said he'd arrange it and left.

Linda was just getting up, and I said to sit back down, I wasn't finished. She reluctantly sat.

"I want to know about David's trip out of the country a couple of months ago. You must have known about it?" I asked.

She looked surprised that I knew, and then she looked evasive but finally said that he took a little vacation with her to the Cayman Islands.

"While the two of you were vacationing, did David by chance happen to visit a couple of banks in the Cayman Islands?" I asked.

She was again surprised and said, "You seem to know more than we thought. Yes, he was trying to get a lead on where Marsha was stashing the money. He found the name of a bank she wrote on a pad at her apartment. It was the Deutsche Bank Limited, a German bank that had a couple of offices in the Cayman Islands. David went there, but found he couldn't get anyone to talk about Marsha's involvement without an account number and pin code, something David couldn't find from Marsha's apartment. He had looked."

That explained David's calls to Germany.

"You had no problem with David sleeping with Marsha?" I asked.

"I did, but it was for us. We would have a good nest egg to start elsewhere. He had been planning on divorcing his wife even before I showed up. We were deeply in love, Mr. Richards. He now knows how much. I want him out of jail even if we lose the money." She paused. "I don't have any money, but if you could help him, I'll try and pay you something."

I've often said I was a sucker for a sob story.

"Let's just see if we can get him out first. Now, does he have any idea who would want to kill Marsha, with or without the money?"

"David has no idea what happened that night. He can't imagine who'd want to kill her."

I handed her the pad and pencil I keep on my desk and told her to write her number and address so I could keep in touch. She did.

I stood. "I have nothing more I need to know. Please, if you hear anything, call me." I handed her my card, and she thanked me. I said I'd return the gun later. She said she didn't feel comfortable with it anyway and left.

About twenty minutes later my phone rang. I answered, and it was Richmond. He said toxicology came back on Paul's blood. He'd been heavily sedated the night of the murder. Alcohol levels were moderate, but he had also been drugged, and it was enough to have kept him out for the night. Richmond said he had a real pain to deal with now, finding the killer since, with this new evidence, he believed Paul was being framed. I asked if Paul was being released, and he said they were going to cut him loose for the moment, too many holes in the story to hold him. I asked when he was getting out. Richmond said in the morning after he checked on a few more details. I said I'd come in to talk to him early, and we finished our call.

OK, the case was getting both interesting and complicated. I sat organizing the details in my head, but that hurt. I went to my pad and paper and wrote an outline of the details, then went to my ample closet, pulled out the dry erase crime board, and started to put the outline on that. I sat back and studied it for a bit, then reached over and dialed Linda Shank's cell number. She answered, and I told her about the drug report and that David was being released in the morning. I said I would be there to talk to him and asked if she could meet me there. She said she would. I hung up. Shortly afterward my cell phone rang. It was Trapper.

"Hey, chief, what's up?" I said.

"Did you name a dog after me?" was all I heard through the phone.

I laughed out loud and said yes.

"You know, Richards, sometimes I think you want to make me nuts. Why did you have to put my name on such a small dog? You couldn't get a pit bull and name it after me, but a Yorkie. Good God, man, it's embarrassing." He was moaning.

"Yeah, but it's a mean Yorkie. How did you find out so quickly? Penny and I just got the dog last night."

"I talked to Buck at Truedell's dog wash business. I came by to check on Becker, and Buck was more than happy to inform me I was now a Yorkie. Damn, it had to be Buck telling me." He was moaning again, then changed the subject. "I see Becker did good on the collar of the informant. What's your take on it?"

"You covered it. He did good. He saw through the guy's demeanor and tripped him up with good interrogation," I said.

"You mean he got lucky." Trapper laughed.

"Luck did have something to do with it, and coincidence. But Barry held up well. Give him some credit."

"Well, the guy's not talking till he gets a deal. Then he says he'll squeal on the hit man and the person who hired him. Maybe this case can get closed soon, and I can put Becker back on the streets."

"You better get Becker into the detectives, or I'll name a poodle after you."

Trapper swore and hung up.

*

Chapter Eighteen

I got home and was greeted by Willy doing a little happy dance just as Penny came out of the hallway from the bedrooms, saw me and did a little happy dance, too. Willy and Penny both danced around the living room. Then she picked the dog up and came to me, planting a big smooch on me, then holding Willy up for a smooch, too. I said, I don't kiss dog lips. She laughed and took Willy to the kitchen. I followed. She said Willy hit all the papers today, not one poop on the floor. She had taken him out in the backyard earlier, and Willy did his business there, too. She was so proud of our new son.

She put the dog down, opened a bag that was on the kitchen counter, and took out a leather looking purse, then came to me, slinging it over my shoulder and head. She reached down, picked up the dog, and inserted him in a pocket in the front of the sling thing. I now understood what it was. A small dog carrier. Willy stuck his head out the front opening and yipped once.

"I saw it at the pet place at Macomb Mall and had to get it. Now we can carry him where ever we go." She smiled and ruffled Willy's little head then kissed me.

"Yes, this is nice, but you get to wear the purse," I said.

"Aren't you confident enough in your masculinity to wear this in public?" She grinned.

"Maybe. I'll try it and see what reaction I get." I grimaced.

"Good, because we need to do some grocery shopping. If you have no big case to work on for the next couple hours, we can go." She went off, got her purse, and offered to drive her car. I looked at Willy staring up at me from the carrier and asked him if there was enough room in there for me to crawl in.

111

Mistress Murders

We got back about an hour and a half later, and Penny was ragging on me about all the women in the store flirting with the dog and me. I said they liked the dog, not me, and it was her idea for me to carry the doggy purse. I secretly enjoyed the attention. She just said next time she'd carry the dog.

We had dinner and went to crash on the couch. I told her about my day, and she told me she had been in the Cayman Islands a few years ago. She said it was beautiful, and she would love to go back there one day. I thought to myself, it may be soon. The three of us packed it off to bed and slept well.

I wanted to be up early to go talk to David Paul, so I set my alarm for 7 a.m. Penny wasn't happy I woke her early, also. Sometimes she can be real cranky in the morning, but not often, only when I wake her early. We got ready for our jobs, and I got Willy prepared for the day then turned on the kitchen TV for him.

I went to my office first to check the answering machine and take another look at my crime board to refresh my memory. I blame old age for my memory lapses. People tend to accept that. I called Linda Shanks, and she said she had been waiting for my call. I said I'd meet her in front of the police station in a half hour, so I closed up and headed west to Madison Heights. I arrived and parked in the lot. Linda was standing by the front doors. I approached her and we exchanged greetings then went inside. I asked the watch Sergeant for Richmond, and he called him. We were told to go on in since I knew where to find him. He was sitting at his desk poring through a pile of paper.

"This crap never ends," he said looking at the mess on his desk. He stood, shook my hand and acknowledged Linda. "I had a little talk with Paul this morning, and he fessed up to the real story of his affair with Webster. He gave me info that matched your statements yesterday," he said to Linda, "so everything is fitting together a little better."

He looked at me. "We now have to find out who drugged Paul and how was it done. And why was this planned so poorly. The keys from the car and the mysterious steak knife—nothing makes sense. Someone must think the police are really stupid to accept this crappy set-up."

I asked if I could talk to Paul, and Richmond agreed. He made a call to have Paul put in interrogation room two and led the way. I asked if he could watch from observation. I wanted to have just Linda and me in the room to make him more at ease. He agreed and opened the door for us then went to the other side of the magic mirror. Linda and I sat for a bit until the door opened and a big guard brought in Paul. As soon as he saw Linda he rushed to her and they embraced. I stood and asked him to sit.

"David, we haven't met yet. I'm Jim Richards, the investigator hired by your wife to tail you." He gave me a scowl then relaxed. "I had nothing against you, just did the job I was hired to do. Now I'm trying to help by finding out who pulled this stunt on you." I paused while that sank into his gray matter. "I need to know everything that happened after you entered the motel room on the night in question. You need to be honest with me, or I can't help you."

Mistress Murders

Linda said, "Dave, tell him everything. It won't bother me. Mr. Richards is a good man and wants to help you." She was apparently remembering how I didn't turn her in for the attempted gun stunt yesterday.

He was quiet for a bit. I gave him the space. Finally he looked at me and said, "We got into the room and we... relaxed." He looked at Linda with an almost embarrassed look, then continued. "Around 10 p.m. I went out to get a bottle of some good scotch and came back. We had a couple of drinks. I was going to see if I could loosen her up a little to get info from her about the money transfers and where she kept the account numbers and pin code for the account. She didn't want to talk about it. I didn't push it at first. I had seen a note on a pad of paper in her apartment one time when I was there, and it had the name of the bank she was dealing with. Couple of months ago Linda and I took a little trip down to the islands, and I made some inquiries about the account but they weren't real open without the numbers. Marsha said she was almost done with the program she inserted in the bank's computers, and in another week all the money would be ours, and we could run off together. I wouldn't have killed her before I got the numbers. That would be real stupid." He went quiet again.

"Why did you two get a motel when Marsha had her own apartment?" I asked.

"Marsha was already out that way, and we agreed to meet at the Gazebo. I suggested that rather than run all the way up to Mt. Clemens, we just get a room nearby. She liked the idea so we went there."

"You say you fell asleep in bed and then woke the next morning in jail. Any idea at all how this happened?"

"After we had a couple of drinks, I was feeling woozy and Marsha suggested we lay down for a while. That's the last I remember of that night."

"Where did you get the booze?" I asked.

"There was a party store near 13 mile and Stephenson Highway. I got it there."

"So the bottle couldn't have been tampered with. How else could you have been drugged?"

He looked lost. "I have no idea, and I don't think Marsha would have done it. What would that accomplish? She wouldn't murder herself and try to make it look like I did it."

"Who else might have wanted her dead?"

"I have no idea, and I'm baffled by how they would have known where we were staying. Only thing I can think of is maybe they followed us, like you did."

I wondered about that, also. I hadn't seen anyone following me or them, so how did someone know where they were?

"Did you or Marsha call anyone from the motel?"

"Not while I was in the room. Marsha may have called someone while I was getting the scotch. I don't know."

"OK, why didn't you just give the information about the embezzlement to the bank dicks? Why go to the trouble to go south and contact the bank? And why the phone calls to Germany?"

Paul looked surprised, then said, "If I had told them of the embezzlement without finding the transfer bank account, I wouldn't have gotten the finder's fee. They would just say they made the paper trail, and I wouldn't be entitled to the fee. I called the bank headquarters in Germany to see if I could get anything from them about the account. I even told them I was a bank official here in the states where we suspected embezzlement involving funds being transferred to their bank. The Germans weren't very friendly."

"OK, a sensitive question here. Why didn't you just hang in with her till the transfers had completed, and then all the money would have been yours? You would have had so much more money that way."

"Mr. Richards, I'm not crooked. I had suspicions that her embezzlements were suspected. If she had completed the transfers the police would have moved in, and we both would be in jail."

I told him I might need to talk more later. I looked at the mirror and said I didn't have anything more to ask.

*

116

Chapter Nineteen

I went into observation leaving Paul and Shank alone in the other room. We could still see them through the mirror glass. I sat down and looked at Richmond. "What's your take on this?" I asked.

"I was hoping you'd figured it out. I'm wearing down on crime fighting. This job is starting to get to me. All the bodies I see, stabbed, shot, hung, mutilated, whatever. All the perps I have to deal with, all the long nights without sleep following a lead that doesn't pan out. Do you know how many cases don't get solved? Way too many. This case is hinky. Nothing makes sense unless there's another crook with his hand in the pie that did this for gain. I was really hoping you could solve it for me." He grinned widely.

"I could solve it then phone it in to the tip hotline and collect a reward." I laughed.

"Yep, taxpayer dollars at work. Want my opinion?" he asked.

"Do I have a choice?"

"Nope. I think we're being set up. Paul knows more than he's saying." Richmond looked at me with weary eyes.

"I was thinking that, too. The whole fiasco is a bit looney tunes. Maybe this is his way to really throw us off him, make it look like a frame job. He probably has the numbers, already got them from Webster and then set up the kill to look like she was murdered without telling anyone where the funds are. He went to the islands to check on the account, and he's now in the clear for the murders. I'm not going to take him off the top of my list of suspects."

"You have suspects?"

"Nope, just him so far." I smiled.

We sat and watched Paul and Shank make kissy face, then Richmond stood and said he was going to cut Paul loose before they started taking their clothes off. I rose and followed him out the door. He took Paul to be processed and released. I told Linda that I would keep in touch and departed the place.

I thought about just leaving the case to the cops. I wasn't getting paid for it, but then the voice in my head said that I had screwed up by not hanging around the motel that night. If I had, this case might have been solved a lot sooner. I guess I felt guilty about it. Now it was personal.

I got in my car and called Trapper. He came on with his usual friendly snarl, and I asked him if Bruce Hardy had been questioned yet.

"The D.A.'s office is dragging their feet. As soon as they get the time to handle menial cases like this, they'll make a deal. Becker's been chomping at the bit all morning. I've never seen him as wired as he's been since he got in this morning."

"I'm at a standstill on my case at the moment. I thought I'd stop by and watch Becker apply the rubber hose to Hardy."

"I'm afraid Becker will kill the guy with the hose. I may have to tie him to the chair during questioning. I haven't heard if Hardy has a lawyer yet, so that should be a surprise. Why don't you stop by and we can chew the fat while we wait?"

I said I was on my way and headed there. I wondered what Buck was up to, so I called him.

"Jimmy, how's your morning going?" he answered happily.

"Lousy so far, but I see brighter skies ahead," I joked. "How are things at doggy central?"

"Good. Mrs. Truedell is feeling much better this morning, probably because she now knows her dog is safe, but I have to remind her that she's not. I talked her into hanging around the house till this blows over. She's not happy, but then she could be dead. Any word about Bruce Hardy?"

"Justice is moving slow this morning, no word. I'm heading over to Clinton Township to watch Becker question Hardy. As soon as they cut a deal with him, hopefully we'll have a name on the person who hired for murder. Until we know and find him, stay on your toes out there."

"No problemo. Me and my .38 are on guard."

Mistress Murders

I said good-bye and hung up. I got to the station and went in the side door straight to the homicide bullpen where I found Trapper talking to Becker. Becker got a big grin when he saw me. I went up to them.

"We just got a deal cut with Hardy and it's a go to question him. We were just heading there," Becker said, then went off to interrogation.

"How much caffeine has he had today?" I asked Trapper.

He laughed and said, too much. We went to the observation room and sat. There was the usual suit in the room with us. I smiled at him and then remembered he was the one who blew his lunch when the Dominatrix murderer blew her brains out over in Roseville precinct. He smiled at me weakly. He must have remembered me, too. Hardy was already seated on the other side of the looking glass. Becker hadn't made his entrance yet.

The interrogation room door opened, and in walked another suit. Must be Hardy's lawyer. Trapper whispered an obscenity then said to me that this lawyer was a pain in the ass. Trapper said he might have to go rescue Becker if things started going south.

"Why would there be any problems? Hardy already got a deal to skate after his testimony. What more can this lawyer do?"

"He's a hard nose. He may make waves over anything. We'll just wait and see."

Becker entered the room and sat across from the two. He asked if Hardy had been given his rights and if he minded the video recording of the interview. Both questions were answered positively by Hardy and his lawyer.

Becker looked at the lawyer and said, "We've already cut a deal with Mr. Hardy for his open testimony, facts on the table, so I don't see anything that you can object to in this questioning. Is there, Mr. Gordy?"

Trapper exhaled a breath and said Becker was going for the throat.

The lawyer sat for a moment then said, "I'm here to see my client gets a fair shake without the crap you cops throw around."

"Well, maybe if your client hadn't crapped on this case, neither he nor you would be here now. So let me do my job, and you can hold the toilet paper."

Trapper made a little applause and said, "That's my boy." I just laughed.

The lawyer sat back and made a wave with his hand, a sort of "it's your show."

"OK, Bruce, we did a little digging. Seems you have quite a criminal record. In and out of Ionia Maximum Correctional Facility, doing time for armed robbery, B & E, attempted murder, and assault on one of your lawyers." Becker glanced at Gordy and smiled. "Seems Mrs. Truedell didn't dig deep enough in your job resume."

"What's that have to do with the inquiry?" Gordy asked.

"Just establishing our footing here. It means that I'll take Bruce's answers with a grain of salt and lots of investigating."

Gordy grumbled a bit then went silent.

"Bruce, yesterday at Truedell's dog grooming business, you admitted to me, two patrol officers and a private investigator that you were involved in the attempts on Truedell's life. Is that correct?"

Hardy looked at his lawyer. Gordy nodded and Hardy mimicked the action.

"You understand that you are to be given immunity on the condition that what you are going to tell us is the complete truth with nothing held back and that this information leads to the arrest of the ring leader of this crime. Is that correct?"

Again with the nods.

"OK, Bruce, spill it from the beginning. Why were you involved, who else were you working with, and who hired you?"

"I just got out of Ionia Correctional and needed a job. I saw a classified ad for a van mechanic in the Macomb Daily, and I answered it. Yeah, I fudged my application, no sense in scaring the old lady right off the bat. She hired me, and I started that week." He paused and took a drink of water from the paper cup on the table that he had asked for earlier. "Around the time Truedell got her dog to start showing and breeding, I got a call, from someone who wanted Truedell dead but didn't want to make it look like she was the victim, just an innocent bystander in a crime. That was important to the caller. It had to be clean. She couldn't appear to be the intended murder victim." He drank again. "I started calling her with threats on the dog, figuring if she got killed in the line of fire it would have looked like collateral damage. I even took a couple of shots at the dog and his big bodyguard to set up the kill. I didn't want them dead. I just needed to start the ball rolling."

"You were a prison buddy with Ed Jackson. Is that why you got hold of him?" Becker asked.

"Yeah, he and I knew each other, and I contacted him to do the kill, but not right away. We had to wait until it was established that the dog was the intended victim. Ed convinced Truedell's last driver to move out of the area. He did, and Ed got hired. We waited about a month until I started the threats. Ed had the bomb gag set up, and it would have worked if that damn bodyguard hadn't queered it and pulled her away from the car. Things started to fall apart after that. I stuck around to see if we could continue the kill, but Ed screwed up with the box. I think he planted it after he was discovered to be the hit man. Just to fuck me over." Another drink.

"Sounds plausible so far. Now who hired you to set up the kill?" Becker sat back and waited.

Hardy sat quietly for a moment then leaned forward and said, "Truedell's son, Mickey."

Chapter Twenty

That caught Trapper and me by surprise. I didn't know Truedell had a son. Of course I knew very little about Truedell.

Becker continued, "How did Mickey know you were the man for the job?"

"Truedell probably doesn't talk much about him, her only son. He's the black sheep of the family. His criminal record is about twice mine. He spent time in Ionia with me, and when he got out, he found out I was working for his old lady and called me to set it up. He went off somewhere in California to establish his alibi. He said he would come back after the deed was done to claim his inheritance. The old lady's worth a good chunk of dough and he said he'd pay me after he got the cash." He took another drink.

"I presume you know how to reach Mickey out in California?"

"Yeah, I got his number. I'm supposed to call him when it's done. Then he'll fly back and play the grieving son."

Becker slid him a pad and pencil and said to write the number down. Hardy did. Becker went to the door, called the guard, and said to escort Hardy back to his cell.

"Hey, I was supposed to walk after I gave up the name," Hardy protested. His lawyer started to open his mouth. Becker pointed a finger at him.

"Don't either of you start on this. The deal was for Bruce to confess, and then we have to arrest the leader before Bruce skates. We're going to need Bruce here to draw Mickey back to Michigan where we can arrest him. Bruce, the D.A. also included a line in that agreement you signed that you were to testify in court on all this. Don't forget that. You were in such a hurry to sign, you didn't wait for your lawyer to look the thing over. If you don't agree to all the terms, you can kiss your immunity and your ass good-bye."

The lawyer shut his mouth and looked at Bruce. "You signed an agreement without me being there? You dumb shit." He stood, got his stuff, told Becker it had been a pleasure, and walked out.

Trapper laughed his head off then said, "Becker may make detective yet. I've never seen him so intimidating."

The guard escorted Bruce Hardy back to his cell. Becker came into observation and sat. Trapper held out his hand to shake. Becker smiled and shook Trapper's hand.

"You did good, Barry." Trapper called him by his first name. That took Becker by surprise, and he smiled.

"I'm going to set up a time for Hardy to call Mickey in California and tell him the car bomb attempt was successful and that Mickey can come back in. We should have a couple officers to meet Mickey at the airport to escort him home," Becker said happily.

"Are you going to tell Truedell that her little boy tried to knock her off?" I asked.

"Damn, I forgot about that. Yeah, I guess I should do it. That will make her day." Becker frowned.

Trapper offered to go with him as a buffer. We all got up, and the two of them went to their unmarked car as I headed to my car and followed.

We arrived at Truedell's home. Buck was sitting on the front porch with the dog, and Mrs. Truedell was resting in a lawn chair in the front yard. Buck came over to the cop car and smiled at me as I got out of my car. Becker and Trapper went over to where Truedell stood. Trapper asked if they could go into her living room to talk. She led them in.

After all were seated, Becker spoke up.

"Mrs. Truedell, Bruce Hardy gave his testimony as to who hired him to attempt your murder." Becker paused. "It turns out that your son Mickey hired him."

Mrs. Truedell looked totally shocked and sat with her mouth wide open.

"That little son of a bitch," she said.

I realized that the son of a bitch was her son, so did that makes her the bitch? I didn't comment.

"Are you sure?" she asked, tearing up.

126

Bob Moats

"We're pretty sure, but won't know definitely until we get him back to Michigan from California. We will be contacting him tomorrow morning to tell him the murder was successful so he'll be coming back thinking he will be claiming his inheritance."

"I want to be there when he arrives. I want to see the look on his face when he sees I'm still alive. Little bastard." She was hot. "I've gone through hell with him since he was young and started out stealing cars. I tried to help him, but he just kept screwing up. Unlike his father, rest his soul, he took to crime rather than making an honest living. The irony is, I already cut him out of the will. He would have gotten nothing after my death. All this would have been for nothing." She asked to be alone so we all got up and left the house.

Outside we all gathered, and the dog started to bark at Trapper.

"Damn dog, what is his problem?" Trapper asked Buck.

"I trained him to bark at your picture." Buck grinned. Trapper gave him the finger and walked away toward his car. Becker told me he got his laptop last night, it was a good deal and the extra money from watching the dog helped. Trapper yelled to Becker to get rolling. They left. I stood next to Buck as the dog licked his face.

"Seems you have a friend. I'm not sure if you should leave Mrs. Truedell until Mickey is in custody. Just hang in for a little while longer to see what happens. I'll let you know."

"Man, that's got to hurt, knowing your own kid would want you dead just for the money," Buck said.

"Yeah, well, be extra supportive of Truedell. She'll need it," I said and then told him I was going to try and solve my murder case. We said our so-longs, and I went to my car.

I went first to a Subway to eat lunch and give Linda Shank a call to see what their plans were. I ate my sub then dialed her number. I got a recording saying the number was no longer in service. I thought that was odd. I had called it earlier that morning and talked to her. I phoned Richmond, told him about the disconnected number and asked if he had a number where Paul could be reached. He gave me the number he had. I called that number and got a computer voice mail saying to leave a message. I have a problem with people who don't identify themselves on voice mail. I never know if I have the right person I'm trying to call. I waited for the beep, identified myself, and gave my number, saying it was important. I actually didn't expect to be called back.

I drove out to see Rene Paul and get her take on David's release. I got to her home and found no one there. I was beginning to feel a little alone in all this and at a loss. While I was there I called her number and got her voice mail. At least she said it was the Paul residence and to leave a message. I did.

I decided to drive over to the motel where Marsha was murdered. The same desk clerk who was on duty the night of the murder was there. I asked if he could look up any calls made from the crime scene room on the night of the murder. Since he was the same person I had talked to about the crime before, he was willing to help. He went through the computer and came up with two numbers that were called from the room. He gave them both to me along with the times they were made. I thanked him and asked if the room was open yet. He said it was, and he took me up to it, let me in, and said to just lock it when I was done.

I didn't know what to expect from the room. It had been cleaned up by the company that cleans crime scenes. They're pretty thorough in cleaning blood, guts and gore from a room. I felt a little uneasy knowing a woman was murdered there, and then I thought about all the motel rooms I had stayed in over the years and how many deaths could have been in those rooms.

I sat on the chair at the little desk and looked at the phone numbers the clerk gave me. I was a bit surprised to find one of them was Linda Shank's number, the now disconnected one. Maybe Paul called her to say he loved her or to set up something. The other number didn't ring any alarms, but the call was made just after 10 p.m. when Paul said he went to get the booze. Could Marsha have called someone? I'd check it when I got back to my office. I studied the room, trying to get a fix on what might have happened that night. I visualized them in the room and what might have gone on. I tried different scenes in my head. Nothing seemed to pop. I left the room, made sure it was locked, then stopped by the office again and slipped the clerk a twenty just to keep him on my side. He smiled and thanked me. I went back to my car and just sat.

*

Chapter Twenty-one

I had no idea what to do next, but finally decided to go back to my office to check on the number and organize my thoughts. I got to my office, went to my computer, fired it up and got on the reverse lookup website for phone numbers. I typed in the number and waited. It came up with nothing, no number found. I picked up my desk phone, hit the star-6-7 buttons, which blocks my number from caller ID and then dialed the number. It rang a couple of times, then a man answered and said hello. I asked if Marsha Webster was there, thinking that might get a reaction. The man said she wasn't there and asked who was calling.

"I'm a private investigator. Do you know when Marsha Webster will be back?" I made a point of saying her whole name again, to see if this person really knew her.

"She doesn't live at this number. May I take a message to give her when I see her?" he asked.

"No message. May I ask who you are?"

"I'm her brother. What's this about?" He sounded concerned.

"I'd rather not discuss it over the phone. It's important, about your sister. Can we meet somewhere?" I asked.

Bob Moats

He was quiet for a moment, and then asked if I knew the Pompo Deli. I was a bit shocked to hear that name again. The classmate killer had sent out emails to his victims from that location. Buck and I went there once to investigate. I told the man on the phone that I knew the place and could be there in thirty minutes. He said, fine, and I told him what I looked like so he'd know it was me. He did likewise.

I sat back and thought about what had just happened. Marsha's brother evidently didn't know she was dead, or this person wasn't her brother, just someone wanting to know what I knew. Either way I would find out shortly. I checked my Glock to be sure it was loaded. I sometimes forget to put the clip in, you know. Old age and poor memory. I headed out, got to the Pompo Deli, and wondered if Stacy still worked there. I went in, and Stacy was there. She looked at me and turned pale.

"God, if you tell me there's another killer here, I'll scream." She gave me a terrified look.

I laughed and said, "No, I'm just here to meet someone. You can relax."

Her shoulders dropped, and she looked relieved then asked if I wanted something to drink. I said a Pepsi and sat at a table with my back to the wall. I hadn't seen anyone matching the description I was given, so I just waited. About ten minutes later a man looking the part came in and saw me. He came over and asked if I was the P.I. I said I was and asked him to sit. Stacy came by, and he asked for a lime soda. I introduced myself. He said his name was Ben Webster.

"You say you're Marsha Webster's brother. When was the last time you talked to her?"

"We talked about four days ago, then she called me late three nights ago but I was out. She left a strange message on my voice mail. I haven't called her back yet. Is she in trouble or something?" He looked genuinely concerned.

I really hated to be the one to tell him of his sister's death. "I have some bad news. Your sister was murdered three nights ago. I'm investigating the murder."

His face dropped, and he went white. He just sat there staring at the wall. I let it soak in a bit then spoke to him.

"I'm sorry to have to be the one to tell you. I guess the police hadn't gotten around to contacting you, or maybe they didn't know about you. Did Marsha talk to you about a man named David Paul?"

"Is he the bastard who murdered her?" he asked quietly.

"It's not proven yet, but he is the main suspect. Did she talk about him?"

"Yes, she said she loved him and they would be going off together soon. She also told me he was married, but was leaving his wife for her. I told her she was stupid for getting involved with a married man. Where is my sister now? I need to see her."

I told him to call the Madison Heights police and talk to Sergeant Richmond who could tell him the details as to the disposition of her body. He took out a note pad and wrote the information down.

"You said she left a message for you the night she was killed. What did she say?" I asked.

"The message was brief. She said she loved me and if anything happened to her, I should go back to our childhood in Ballywick. It was a reference to a childhood game we used to play. We would hide this puzzle box in our parents' backyard, a huge yard filled with trees and bushes, and the other person would have to find it. We called our backyard Ballywick, sort of a fantasyland to us. The puzzle box contained a riddle that had to be solved in order to win the prize, usually chocolate cookies or M & Ms." He was silent for a minute. "Well, something has happened to her. What do I do about her message?"

"Is this Ballywick still there?"

"Yes, my other sister lives there now. Oh, God, I have to tell Helen about this. It'll kill her. Marsha and Helen were very close."

"Helen is the other sister?"

"Yes, she was the oldest. Marsha was the baby of us three." He was starting to tear up.

"Do you think, after you see your sister and get arrangements made, we could try to figure out what she meant by her message? It sounds like she may have hidden the puzzle box again for you to find. It may help to find her killer." I hoped he would cooperate.

"Of course, anything to help. I'll call you when I'm free, and we can go search the yard."

Mistress Murders

I didn't want to press him, what with just finding out his sister was murdered. I thanked him, paid for our drinks, and gave him my card. He said he would call in a day or so. I asked him not to say anything to anyone about Ballywick until we had a chance to check it out. He agreed and went off to his car. I stood in the parking lot taking in the warm air and watching him go. I was tired and the day was at a standstill, so I decided to head home.

I got home to find Penny swinging around her stripper pole and Willy zipping around it trying to follow her. I laughed, and she suddenly saw me and stopped.

"I didn't hear you come in. Sneaky." She smiled and kissed me. "I was getting my exercise and taking Willy for his walk around the pole." She was sweaty from her romp on the pole, and I said so. Willy was bouncing at my feet so I picked him up and nuzzled him. He yipped and tried to lick my face.

Penny ran off to the other room, leaving me alone on the porch. Willy and I sat playing for a short time till Penny came back to the room wearing a beaded headband, the kind that a Native American female would wear. I was puzzled at first by that and asked where she got it.

She said she had representatives of local Native American tribes on her show today. They made her an honorary member and gave her the headband. They told tales of their lives and showed a lot of items that they used years ago to survive the wilds. I said that she needed a buckskin thong to go with the headband. She told me to behave, took off the headband, and went to put it on the mantle in the family room.

The three of us plopped down on the couch and I told her of my exploits of the day. She was happy to see things were shaping up in the Truedell case and sorry to hear about Marsha's brother finding out the hard way about her death.

"Well, if I hadn't told him, the cops would have. Anyway, I have a new thread in the case. Hopefully Marsha planted some good info that I can use."

"I love riddles and searches in a fantasy garden. Can I come?" she asked like a little girl begging for an ice cream cone.

"Well, depends on if you're available and when he can set it up, but I see no problem with it. We could always use an extra pair of eyes."

She sat back and smiled. I kissed her cheek and said, "I've been afraid to have you along on my cases because of the attempts on your life in the past, but I guess I can't always be worried. You're a big girl. You proved that with the kidnapper in the van in Vegas. I still picture you with the pipe in your hand banging on him, yelling that he was a son of a bitch." I grinned at her.

"Yes, that was scary, but fun. Remember, I learned those protective moves from the karate guy on my show," she said with her chin up.

I remembered all right. I'd arrived home that day and she'd tossed me around the backyard. I knew she could handle herself, and now I wanted to take her along. She could protect me.

We made and ate dinner and, accompanied by Penny's complaints, I still snuck Willy a few bits of food. I did catch Penny "accidentally" dropping a piece of hot dog. I didn't say anything.

*

Chapter Twenty-two

We were in bed when my cell phone rang at 6:45 a.m. It was Becker. He asked if I wanted to be in on the phone call to Mickey from Bruce. I said I did. He told me they were going to call around 11 a.m. because of the three-hour difference in time between Michigan and California. I said I'd be there and hung up. I rolled over to Penny but found Willy between us. I lifted him, set him on the edge of the bed, and snuggled up to my girl.

She said, still half asleep, "Willy, stop that, be a good dog and go back to sleep." I barked in her ear and she turned her head to face me. She kissed my nose and said, "Bad doggy."

I was getting myself together in the bathroom with the dog running around my feet When Penny walked in, dropped her robe, and went straight to the shower. She turned, gave me a smile and asked if I wanted to soap her up. I said she should ask the dog. She pouted, and then I dropped my robe.

We had breakfast and headed out to our jobs. I got to my office and checked my machine. No calls from David Paul. I wondered if he'd skipped town. I sat in my squeaky chair and called the number Richmond gave me for him. Again I got the answering machine. I called Rene Paul's number. Rene wasn't answering, either. Strange. I had no other number to call so I just sat back and waited for the time to arrive when I could go see Bruce call Mickey in California.

My cell phone rang. Caller ID said it was Richmond. I answered, and he asked if I had heard from David Paul. I said I hadn't been able to reach him. He replied that they couldn't, either. I said he should check all airline flights to the Cayman Islands to see if he was heading south. He said that was a good idea, said good-bye and hung up.

Now I was wondering about the innocence of Paul and Linda both. I got up and decided to go bug Trapper before the call.

I headed to the station, got to his desk, and he wasn't there. I sat in his extra chair and put my feet up on his desk. About five minutes later, I heard someone come up behind me complaining about who they let in this place. He came up, shoved my feet off his desk, and sat.

"Are you bored this morning?" he asked. "I can let you rest in a cell if you'd like."

"Becker called me at an ungodly hour to tell me Bruce was making the call this morning. He asked if I wanted to observe."

Mistress Murders

"Good old Becker. He's still wired. I hope this case is over soon, or he'll have a stroke."

Becker came in, said he had a phone set up in interrogation room four and it was wired for recording. We all went down there and a big guard brought in Bruce, sitting him in front of the phone. The suit was there, too, this time on the questioning side of the glass. We all sat around the table, and Becker took command.

"Bruce, we went over this in your cell. You know the routine. Don't disappoint me, or you will not see the light of day for at least a year. I'm going to dial, and then you will take the phone and tell Mickey what I told you to tell him. Don't even stray one word from the script. Understand?"

Bruce looked at Becker with weary eyes and just nodded. Becker asked the electronic tech detective on the recording equipment if he was ready, and the guy nodded.

"Good. If everyone's ready, here we go." He reached for the phone, signaled the tech guy, and then he dialed the number. It started ringing; we could all hear it through the speakers of the recording equipment. Becker handed the phone to Bruce, and he listened.

"Yeah, this better be good," came a voice on the phone.

"Mickey, it's Bruce. The deed is done. You're an orphan, man," Bruce said into the phone.

"Fan-fucking-tastic!" Mickey yelled. "I don't even want to know how you did it, just say she's dead!"

"Your old lady's dead. You wanted it, we did it. When you coming back? I can use that money you promised for the hit."

"I'll pack my bags and be on the next flight to Detroit in the morning. Meet me coming off of Northwest at Metro, whenever it says they have a morning flight coming in. I don't know what flight, so just watch for me early in the morning. Good work, man, I'm proud of you. See you tomorrow." He hung up.

"Very good, Bruce. Your part is done. When we have Mickey in custody, we'll arrange with the D.A. for your release," Becker said and then called the guard to take Bruce back to his cell.

I looked at Trapper and said, "That was exciting. Now what do we do for the rest of the day?" He grinned and got up to go out, but stopped and turned to Becker.

"Barry, you're doing well. Now you have to contact the airport police at Metro to let them know of your bust, just so there are no surprises from the rent-a-cops at Metro." Becker nodded and headed out to make his call.

Trapper looked at me and asked if I wanted a coffee or something. I said, something if he was buying. We went to the iron cafeteria. Trapper put his money in the slot and got a coffee, then fed the machine again and told me to take my pick. I took a hot chocolate. We went to sit in the lounge, well, the small room that served as storage and a lounge.

"I'll have Becker call Truedell later to tell her of our trip to Metro. Buck can drive her there. She can't come in our cars. I'll take my issued car, and you can come along if you want. Just be here if you want to go." He sat back and blew on his coffee. My chocolate was too hot to drink, so I blew on it, also.

He asked me about my case, and I told him all the details up to the unanswered calls to Paul. He said they were probably flying the coop. Then he asked who was paying me. I told him no one. He snickered and said, a pro-bono job, eh? I told him it was personal to me now, that I had to make amends to Marsha.

My cell phone rang, and the caller ID just had a number, no name. I answered. It was Ben Webster, Marsha's brother.

"Yes, Ben, what can I do for you?" I asked.

"You can help catch the son of a bitch who murdered my sister," he said quietly. "I was just at the morgue and viewed her. I want justice done for her. This is a priority. If you think the Ballywick message may help, I want to find out. Can we meet there?"

I looked at my watch. It was just around noon, and Penny would be home. I asked where the place was and he gave me directions and the address. It was in Harrison Township, not far from our house, so I could swing by and get Penny and be there in an hour. I told him I would meet him there and that he shouldn't do anything till I got there. He said he had to break the news to his sister, so he would be busy till I got there.

I called Penny, and she said she would be ready to be picked up and asked if the dog could come. I looked at

Trapper who was listening in on my conversation and said, sure, we'll bring little Willy with us. He gave me the finger.

I drove out to our house and found Penny waiting by the door with Willy in his mobile pouch. We drove up to Harrison Township, and I found the house. I drove in the long front drive and parked behind a Jeep Cherokee.

Penny and I got out just as Ben was coming through the front door of the pleasant Tudor style home, all done in large stone and half timbered. It looked like a fantasy house. Ben came to me with hand extended. I took it and introduced Penny. He recognized her from TV and said it was an honor to meet her. She blushed.

"My sister Helen is too upset to join us. We can start if you're ready."

"Lead the way, and if you could explain the game to us, we can get started."

Penny had Willy in his carrier, and she looked excited to be helping. We went out to the backyard. It was huge. Ben said there were five acres of land. It had been a great place for them to play when they were children. There were a couple groves of small trees and hedges traveling around the yard making a maze. There were small gardens of colorful flowers and plants, and in the center of the yard was a small pond with actual goldfish.

Ben said the game basically was to find the puzzle box and then read the riddle in it. He hoped Marsha had inserted the name of her killer in it. I told him that was unlikely but whatever she did put in it might help.

I said we should spread out and search. I asked what the box looked like. He said it was about two inches square, light brown wood, varnished, and it had a checkered pattern on it. He said he checked the shelf in the house where they usually kept it, and it wasn't there.

We decided the most effective way to split up, and we all went our separate ways. We searched for about an hour and met back by the pond.

"I haven't seen anything like you described," I said. Penny agreed, and Ben looked frustrated. I asked where in the past they usually hid it. He said he'd checked all those places and found nothing. Penny went to the pond to admire the fish and suddenly called us over. She pointed to an object on the bottom of the pool. It was the box wrapped in a plastic bag.

*

Chapter Twenty-three

Ben went to get a net on a long pole and fished the box out. He held the net to me, and I removed the box. He tossed the pole aside and came over to me and Penny. I had already torn open the plastic bag and was studying it, then I handed it to Ben and said I was sure he knew how to open it. He took it and started to push and pull on the sides. Finally the box slid open. He took out a piece of paper and handed it to me.

I looked at the paper. It had handwriting on it. I read aloud:

"Big brother Ben, the longitude and latitude of the place where you will find the reward is 42 degrees, 386 minutes and 34 seconds south, by 82 degrees, 498 minutes and 43 seconds west. The prize is open to you by giving the command AEIOS. Thank you for all you've done and for being there for me, brother. I love you, Marsha."

I asked Ben if they had a computer in the house. He said, of course, that they were a family of computer nerds. He took us to a room that I had to drool over. It was equipped with three computers—two desktops and a laptop—various printers and scanners and an assortment of extra peripherals. He said his sister Helen, who was lying down, had a web consulting business.

Ben pointed to one of the desktops, and I sat. The computer was already running. I clicked on the web browser icon, waited and then went to Google maps. I typed in the latitude and longitude in the search bar and hit enter. We waited, and the thing responded with a "not found" reply. I sat back and wondered why. I did a search on just the first two sequence of numbers, the degrees and minutes, and hit the enter button. Same reply, nothing.

I tried entering just the hours, and the map came up in Michigan around Macomb County, but an exact point on the map wasn't given. I knew the coordinates for my parents' house. They were in the 42 and 82 degree area, but I realized the 386 and 498 minutes couldn't be right.

Mistress Murders

They were too high. This was not longitude and latitude. I spoke my thoughts out loud to Penny and Ben. Penny was looking over my shoulder and said that maybe the numbers could be the bank account numbers Marsha was hiding in her message. I had a flash of reality. Penny might have hit it. I jumped up and kissed her, then explained to Ben the painful truth about Marsha embezzling money from her bank and that these numbers could be the offshore account numbers the police needed. Ben was shocked by his sister's criminal activity and said he wanted nothing to do with it. I expressed my regrets. He said to just find the killer, and he would be happy.

He led us to the front door. We thanked him for his help, and I said I would keep him informed as to my progress. Penny and I got into the car, and I leaned over, kissed her cheek, and said, "Good job catching that."

She asked if she was now on the payroll. I laughed and said, don't count on it, that I wasn't getting paid for this case. She gave me a strange look and asked why. I explained my personal reasons, and she accepted it. She did mention the finder's fee if we got the bank account for them. I had thought about that.

As we were heading back to our house, my cell phone rang. It was Richmond. "Richards, you heard or seen David Paul or Linda Shank at all today?"

"Nope, I've been busy on other matters. I was going to go later today to the address that Paul gave you."

"Don't bother. He's not there. The place is deserted. Looks like they came and got a few things and then dropped off the face of the earth. I don't know what kind of a warrant to put out on them, other than missing material witnesses, although Paul is still a prime suspect. I guess I'll go with that. I did check the airlines. Nothing is popping under either name. If you see or hear anything, call me."

I said I would and hung up. I looked at Penny and asked, "How would you like a return trip to the Cayman Islands?"

She mustered up a big grin and asked, when do we leave? I said I had something to do tomorrow morning then we could plan on heading down. I dropped her off at the house after exchanging a quick tonsil search with her and a hug for Willy, then I headed over to Madison Heights to see Richmond.

Richmond had nothing more to say other than they couldn't find either Paul or Shanks. He said that Rene Paul hadn't heard from her husband since he was released. She wasn't even aware he was out till Richmond told her.

I told Richmond that I would be taking a short trip to the Cayman Islands to check on something involving the missing funds and would give him a call when we got back. He just said, Bon Voyage, and I departed the place.

It was 2:30 p.m., and I had nothing important to do till the morning when we would bring in Mickey Truedell. I headed back to the house. Penny was relaxing on the couch with Willy, watching a video tape she had from her last trip to the Cayman Islands. She started the thing over, and we both watched. The place where she'd stayed was beautiful. I was sure it was the tourist section of town, made to look happy and pretty for the people coming to spend their vacation money on luxuries and trinkets hand-made by the locals after they removed the Made In China labels.

After it was over, I said that I was taking my favorite girl out for a nice dinner to celebrate getting closer to the missing funds. Poor Willy was not happy to be blocked in the kitchen again as we departed. While we were enjoying our meal, Becker called me to say the earliest flight into Detroit from Northwest Air was 7:45, and if I wanted to be there, I should meet Trapper around 6 a.m. so we could all head down to Metro. I thanked him and said I would be there.

After we got back to the house I called Buck about tomorrow morning. I told him when and where he and Truedell should meet us to go to Metro. He said they'd be there and said that Truedell was anxious to see her evil progeny get busted. I laughed and said I'd see him then.

Penny and I did our usual nightly TV, beer and chips ceremony. Willy was comfy on a pillow Penny put on the couch for him. We finished up the night and went to bed. I warned Penny I was setting my alarm for about 5 a.m. She grumbled that I better not wake her. I didn't.

By 5:30 a.m. I was driving over to Clinton Township police headquarters thinking about the Cayman Islands and hoping the numbers we had worked out to an account. I didn't call the banks down there because I didn't want to tip anyone's hand that we had the numbers, I wanted to track the account down to the destination and return the fund myself so no one else could claim the finder's fee. I was going to be very protective of my reward. I wondered if Paul already had the numbers and was already there, taking it all. But then I thought that if Marsha had put the numbers in the puzzle box, maybe she hadn't shared them with anyone else. Too much to think about, but a vacation in the sunny tropics with my favorite girl would be nice even if the numbers didn't pan out.

I drove into the cop shop and saw Trapper and Becker standing by Trapper's unmarked car. I parked and came to them, saying my good mornings and listening to Trapper growl about it being too ungodly early to go on a bust. Becker went over to one of the two patrol cars that would go with us. They were taking a small army to be sure they got Mickey. Just then Buck drove in with Truedell but without the dog. Buck came over to me and told me it would be too much trouble at the airport getting the dog in, so he convinced Truedell to leave Benny with the housekeeper. I said that was good, and then we all got into our little caravan and drove over to I-94 freeway to go south to Detroit Metro Airport.

In about an hour we pulled into the airport service area where the captain of the Metro security police told us to park. We took an elevator up to the security offices of the airport, and Becker conferred with the captain about our plans. He assigned a couple of his people to be sure we had no problems and had one of the officers take us to the arrival gates of Northwest to wait.

Becker stationed his uniformed officers around the perimeter of the door that the arriving passengers would come through, hopefully including Mickey. Becker asked one of the airport police if he could check to see if Mickey Truedell was on the passenger list. The officer went to the boarding counter and inquired. He turned back to Becker and nodded. The tension was high as the huge airplane was pushed into position for unloading. The enclosed ramp was moved out to the door which opened on the side of the plane, and then the passengers were allowed to come out. We all stood back, watching for Mickey. Becker gave everyone a copy of Mickey's booking photo, but it was a couple years old and he could have changed his appearance. It was good we had Mrs. Truedell with us. She'd recognize him no matter what he looked like.

I have a gripe when I watch cop shows on TV or at the movies. The police always start to call to the suspect when they are about twenty feet or more away from the guy they want to collar. This gives the suspect plenty of time to scoot away, starting the exciting chase through the neighborhood. That's showbiz. I knew Becker and Trapper were smart enough to wait till Mickey was right on them before springing on him. What we hadn't counted on was Mrs. Truedell. As soon as Mickey stepped off the ramp, she started yelling at him, calling him a bastard.

Mickey looked totally shocked and then ran back up the ramp.

*

Chapter Twenty-four

The disembarking passengers made it difficult for the army of officers to follow Mickey as he ran back to the plane. He stopped just short of the door, squeezing through the opening between the plane and the ramp. He swung from a bar on the side of the ramp and dropped down to the ground. The officers tried to follow, but their gun belts and other attachments to their uniforms prevented them from getting through the small opening. Becker and Trapper saw what was happening from the huge windows looking out over the tarmac. Becker yelled to one of the airport security to get his men out there to see if they could stop him. The officer got on his walkie-talkie and reported the incident.

Mrs. Truedell stood with her mouth open, looking chagrined and aware of what she had done. Buck said that they should just get the hell out before Mickey somehow got back around to her. They headed back to the security office. I just stood watching them go. Trapper and Becker had already run off to see if they could get to the ground. I wasn't feeling like running all over the airport looking for a man who I was sure was well away by that time.

I headed towards the security offices, figuring I could ride back with Buck if need be. I met Buck in security, and he just stood there looking helpless. Mrs. Truedell was seated, wiping her eyes with a tissue. I said, what's done is done, but Mickey would surely be found. The whole airport police staff and Becker's men were all over the place looking for him. We just sat waiting.

Mistress Murders

About a half hour later, Trapper came in with the airport officers. He didn't look happy.

"Mrs. Truedell, that was something I'm sure you didn't plan, but it didn't help. We lost him. Now we will put out an APB and, hopefully, the local cops can nab him. Is there any place he might go that you know of?"

"No, I don't know his friends or anywhere he would go to. I'm really sorry I did that. I was just so pissed at him, I couldn't help myself when I saw him." She sat back looking upset.

"Well, we will find him. Becker's on the horn checking with Bruce Hardy to see if he may know where Mickey hangs in town. I'm sure Bruce doesn't want Mickey on the loose looking for him after he snitched, so he'll cooperate with us."

Trapper turned to me and said, "Nothing much we can do here. One of the airport police said that a man fitting Mickey's description grabbed a cab out of the airport. Becker's checking with the cab company and will be taking the patrol cars to the destination the cab was going. He'll keep us informed, but we should head back up and get Mrs. Truedell home." Trapper thanked the Captain of the airport security, and we left the office.

Buck and Truedell were in Buck's car following Trapper and me up the freeway when Trapper's cell phone rang. He answered and listened for a bit then hung up.

"Becker said that the cab that took the person described as Mickey was told to go up to Mt. Clemens. No specific address was given. The cab passenger said he would tell the driver where to go once they were there. Becker also said that, according to Bruce, Mickey had friends in Mt. Clemens, some bad friends. We're going to get some armed troops to go in there and inquire if they know Mickey's whereabouts." He smiled. I knew he liked armed attacks on criminal hangouts.

We got back up to Clinton Township, and Buck waved to us as he headed over to Truedell's home. I asked Trapper if it would be a good idea to have a couple of cars go there to guard in case Mickey decided to go home. He thought about it, then got on his radio and called for at least one car to go there. He smiled at me and said, budget cuts. I thought about those budget cuts back when we were guarding Penny during the classmate murders case.

Trapper said that Mickey had about a half hour head start on us. He gathered as many uniforms as he could and called the Macomb County Sheriff's office who were patrolling Mt. Clemens since the city police force was disbanded due to economic crunch. He informed them his team was after a fugitive who fled from Metro airport and was presently somewhere in Mt. Clemens. The Sheriff he talked to said that they would cooperate with them in the apprehension, just let them know where and when.

Trapper called Becker and asked if he had an address yet. Becker said the cab driver was told to drop Mickey off at the county building in downtown Mt. Clemens. Becker said that Bruce didn't know the house address offhand, so we would need to take him there. Becker said he was on his way back and would be there in about twenty minutes. Trapper briefed his team, and when Becker arrived, he got Bruce from his cell and everyone headed up Groesbeck to Harrington then over to Gratiot Avenue following Bruce's directions. I followed in my car since I didn't want to get left somewhere if things went bad.

The train of cop cars went north up Gratiot to Cass Avenue and pulled up to a house that Bruce said was where the gang usually hung out. The armed and armored police and a couple of the sheriff's deputies were dispersed to surround the house. Becker and Trapper in Kevlar vests went to the front door and banged, yelling for someone to open up. No response. The battering ram was brought out, and the cops all piled into the house. They found a couple of grubby looking men stoned out on mattresses on the floor amid squalor in the living room. The men looked shocked to see all the cops and held their hands up.

The team checked all the rooms in the house and found a couple of women who looked like they might be hookers sleeping in a back bedroom. The big bust came when they checked the basement and found a small meth lab. Becker conferred with Trapper and then told the sheriff that they could take the bust since all he wanted was the fugitive. Upon questioning, the two men both admitted to knowing Mickey but said he had already been there and left and they didn't know where he went.

Trapper pulled back his men and let the sheriff take the lead on the bust. Becker gave a copy of Mickey's photo to the sheriff and asked if he could be on the lookout for him. Then we all headed back to the precinct.

I sat at Trapper's desk as he made calls for warrants on Mickey. He finished and sat back.

"Well, this has been one hell of a day. Done a lot and accomplished nothing. I can't blame Becker. He did what he could with what he had. I'm happy with his work." Trapper smiled and dropped his head on the desk like he was going to sleep.

I chuckled and said, "I hope you let Barry know he did good. It will help his confidence."

Trapper kept his eyes closed while he replied, "He has enough confidence now. He needs more experience, but he'll be all right."

It was noon, and I was getting hungry. I asked if Trapper wanted to go out and get something to eat. He said, thanks, but he had a ton of paperwork to do. I said I was going to Burger King; I was getting tired of subs. I left. He still had his head on the desk. I went to my car just as I saw Becker drive in. I went over to his car.

"Hey, Barry, any word on Mickey?" I asked.

He looked distressed. "None. He just disappeared. We'll put Bruce back in his cell. He definitely doesn't want to be out on the streets with Mickey loose. All we can do now is wait."

"Well, just to let you know, Trapper said you did good despite what he may say to you, so remember what I said."

Becker got that silly grin on his face and went off to the building. I went to my car, drove to the Burger King on Gratiot Avenue and ate lunch, then thought about what I would do now. The dog show was tomorrow. I wondered if Truedell was still going to enter Benny. I decided to drive out to Truedell's and see what they were up to.

I got to the driveway, saw Buck's car, pulled next to it, and went up to the door just as it opened. Buck stood there smiling at me.

"Hey, Jimmy, find the bad guy yet?" he asked.

"Nope, he's still on the loose, so be alert. Where's the cop that Trapper assigned here?"

"He parked his car out back and is watching from the garage. He told me you were driving in."

We went in to where Mrs. Truedell was resting, and I asked her if she was still going to enter the dog show tomorrow. She perked up, said that she almost forgot about that, and got up, calling for Benny who was in the kitchen eating his lunch. Truedell went out of the room, still calling the dog. I looked at Buck. He shrugged and commented on the events of the morning.

"Quite a day. Mrs. Truedell is really on edge with Mickey out there somewhere. Think it's wise to let Truedell out for the show?" Buck asked.

"I think that Mickey won't bother with it. I'm sure he doesn't even know about the show, so it's unlikely he'll try anything. Besides he went to a lot of trouble to make Truedell's death look accidental. He won't try to commit the murder himself."

I hoped.

Chapter Twenty-five

I decided to hang around Truedell's place for a while. Buck and I sat in the back yard watching Truedell and the dog trainer she called in to put Benny through his paces. The dog did real well running around a circle, jumping hurdles, and going through hoops. I'd never been to a dog show before, so it was all Greek to me. The trainer complimented Mrs. Truedell on Benny's abilities and said he should do real well in the show tomorrow. They worked for another hour, then Mrs. Truedell said she was getting a little tired and thought Benny was doing well enough to quit for the day. The trainer thanked her; collected his fee and left. Buck and I were at the front of the garage talking to the cop guarding the property when the trainer came around the corner. I stopped him and asked if he really thought the dog would do well. He said that he had a chance, provided the other dogs didn't do better. He smiled and left.

It was around 5 p.m., and we watched a car drive in and pull up next to us. It was Becker. He got out and came over with that big kid grin he had.

"Hey guys, I decided I was going to stay around here for the night, if Mrs. Truedell doesn't mind," he said.

Buck said Truedell would love to have more cop company, that she was on pins and needles since the airport. Becker told the other cop that his relief would be out shortly.

"Barry, are you here on your own or were you assigned to come out?" I asked.

He smiled sheepishly and said he was on his own and hoped Mickey would show up, that he wanted first crack at him. I said I hoped Mickey would show up for him and told them I was heading home to rest and play with my puppy. Buck said, wouldn't Penny be jealous? I said, who'd he think I was going to play with? Later I'd play with the dog.

I drove out to the house. When I got there I heard Jamaican music. I thought I might just turn around and go back to Truedell's, but the door opened and out popped Penny in a sarong. At least she didn't corn row her hair.

"Hello, Mon. I be waiting for you," she said in a poor imitation of Rasta lingo. She pulled me into the house where I was greeted with a living room full of bright light strings of pineapples and streamers. I half expected a pig roast in the middle of the living room. She said it was out in the back yard. Willy had a silly little lei around his neck. He wasn't fighting to get it off, I noted.

She pushed me back on the couch and did a hula dance. I said she was on the wrong island, and she said to shut up and enjoy the show. I did.

As I sat there watching her and Willy doing their dances, I thought about how marriage experts all say that a healthy relationship has spice in it. I thought about all the men in the world who came home to a wife slaving over a stove and bitching about bills, kids and how the husband never paid attention to her. I came home to a wacky woman who changed every time, playing different roles and doing it for me. I thought about the time she dressed up like Marilyn Monroe for me. How many men could say that?

I stood, grabbed her, and held tight. She made a little squeal and asked what was I doing. I just said, loving you. Hell, even with my bad back, I lifted her in my arms and carried her to the bedroom. We didn't come out till morning, and Willy wasn't allowed in with us.

It was a beautiful Saturday morning. I had a big breakfast with Penny and Willy and announced that we were going to a dog show today. She asked if it was the one from her guest on her show last week. I said it was. The Greater Detroit Dog Breeders Society AKC sanctioned dog show. Mrs. Truedell was entering her dog, and I thought it would be a good learning experience for Willy to watch. Penny loved the idea, and we got ready to go. I told Penny I would wear the doggy purse. She said it was just my way of attracting women. I grinned and said, "Who me?" She tossed me the carrier and said she would drive.

We left, got to the Pontiac Silverdome and fought the traffic into the parking lot. We had to park out in the boonies, and I commented on how this dog show must be a big deal to have attracted so many people. We got to the gates and found out there was also a big time wrestling match going on in the other half of the now separated arena. We paid our entrance fee, and I asked the ticket seller if dogs got in free. She said they did. Willy had his head out of the front of the carrier and was yipping at all the people. I don't like barking dogs, but Willy's yip was so cute I didn't complain. Penny took my hand as we walked through the crowd of people gathered around the center ring of champion dogs all waiting their turn to show off. I finally spotted Buck and Truedell, and we headed in their direction.

As we approached, I saw Becker standing behind the two of them watching the crowd. Penny and I came up and said our howdies. Becker admired little Willy. So did Buck who hadn't seen the dog in person yet. Mrs. Truedell showered Willy with love and kisses until Benny started to bark. She apologized to him and went to sit.

"Any problems so far?" I asked Becker.

"Nope. It was a quiet night with no reports on Mickey's whereabouts. Going good so far." He sounded relieved. "I did contact local police and stadium security about the situation and gave them copies of his picture. If he shows up here, we'll be ready."

"You're a good man, Charlie Brown." I laughed. He looked at me kind of funny, then he laughed, too.

The dog show started with the national anthem, and then the president of the Dog Breeders Society announced the opening of the show. He introduced various members of the society, the officials of the AKC, and their judges. The show started off with large breed dogs. We watched the various canines go through their paces. Eventually all the dogs were put on display for the judges to examine. They walked up and down the lineup and then announced their decisions as to the three top winners. All this took about an hour, then they went on to another category. I imagined that Mrs. Truedell was getting nervous waiting.

Buck stood behind her watching the crowd for Mickey's face. I didn't think he'd be crazy enough to show up. Penny had Willy up by the partition that kept the audience off the field. She was narrating and pointing things out to Willy. After about an hour and a half, it was Benny's turn on the field. Mrs. Truedell took him out proudly and put him through his paces. Then the lineup came, and the judges examined all the terriers standing erect for them. The judges conferred with each other, then the head judge came out and announced the winners. Benny and Mrs. Truedell came in second. Not bad. Mrs. Truedell beamed as they gave her the ribbon.

She came off the field, handed Buck the leash, and attached the ribbon to her purse. She slung that purse over her shoulder so the ribbon was displayed on the front. She then took the leash back, and we headed to our cars. Buck said he was parked closer to the front, and I told him we would all meet at Truedell's place and celebrate. As we parted, I looked back and saw that Buck had a funny expression on his face. I stopped Penny and we watched as Buck, Mrs. Truedell and some man wearing a low slung baseball cap started to walk in a direction away from the parking lot.

We began following the three of them while I got on my cell phone, called Becker, and asked where he was. Becker said he was with stadium security at the main gate. They said someone fitting Mickey's description had entered the gate about an hour ago. I said I was watching him with Truedell and Buck. I gave him our location and direction. He said he'd have security come with him. I told

Mistress Murders

Penny what was going on and said Mickey must have a gun on Truedell, otherwise Buck would have killed him already.

The three of them went off to a door on the side of the arena across from the snack counters. I called Becker again to give him our latest location, but he and three stadium cops came up just then. He quickly introduced us all and we went through the door with the stadium cops leading the way. Becker and I had our guns drawn and ready. I realized Penny was behind me and told her it was too dangerous to follow. She got insistent and said she was going to follow anyway and that she'd keep her head down. I didn't have time to argue so I just went on.

We went down a long, dark, dank hallway, and I spotted something ahead low to the floor. It was Benny. Penny saw the dog, too, and rushed up to get its leash. She bent down to calm the dog who was shaking badly. Willy, in his pouch, was close enough to lick Benny's nose, and Benny returned the favor. I figured Mickey told Truedell to get rid of the dog which was probably slowing them down. I told Penny to bring the dog, and we headed further down the hall. I asked the stadium cop closest to me where the hallway lead to. He said it went around to the other side of the arena where the wrestling matches were going on.

I had a bad feeling about that.

Chapter Twenty-six

Ahead of us Buck was running followed by Mrs. Truedell and Mickey. They came to another door. Mickey herded them through the door into a throng of people all screaming and yelling at the wrestlers who were smashing each other in the ring. Mickey told his prisoners to stop. He surveyed the room, spotted an exit sign on the other side, and pushed them to go on. A few minutes later my group came out the same door, but we couldn't see them. They had blended into the crowd. After a moment of getting our bearings, I heard a commotion. People were yelling that Hulk Hogan was in the arena. I asked one of the cops if Hogan was supposed to be there. He said no. I knew what was happening and told everyone to follow. I went in the direction of the noise.

I came around the side and saw Buck being thronged by admirers who didn't realize he wasn't Hogan. I couldn't see Truedell or Mickey, so I figured they had been split off from Buck by the crowd. I got to him just as a wrestler got up in Buck's face about something. The two of them started to fight, and the crowd moved back to watch. We made our way over to the two of them, and Becker and I held our guns on the wrestler as the stadium guards pulled him off Buck. The wrestler saw our guns and dropped to the ground with his hands on his head. I looked at Becker and said, he must know the position. Buck was growling and said to me that Mickey was heading to the exit. We all ran off in that direction. The crowd was going nuts over the little show they'd just witnessed.

Mistress Murders

We got to the door, went through it, and found Mrs. Truedell sitting on the ground. She was unhurt and I asked where Mickey was. She said as they came through the door, he was spotted by two stadium police standing outside the door. Mickey panicked, pushed her at the cops, causing her to fall, and ran off down that hall. She pointed in the direction he'd gone. Buck and I got Mrs. Truedell on her feet, and I asked why Mickey hadn't fired his gun at the cops. She said she didn't know, but Buck said he thought that Mickey didn't have a gun, just his hand in his pocket, that he didn't want to take the chance of Mrs. Truedell getting hurt. Buck didn't pull his gun because there were too many people around and someone could have gotten hurt if Mickey was armed. One of the cops with us got a call on his walkie-talkie that the suspect left the building and was heading out to the back fields around the stadium, over to North Opdyke Road. He said he'd alert the Auburn Hills, Pontiac and Utica police to be on the lookout.

Becker was steaming since Mickey got away again. Penny came up behind me. I had forgotten about her in the excitement. She handed Benny's leash to Mrs. Truedell and said she was excited by that little jaunt around the stadium. I told her to hold that thought. We asked the stadium cops if they could escort us to the parking lot. They called up a golf cart, drove around the side of the building and dropped us off at Buck's car. We thanked them, and I gave them one of my cards with the request that, if they saw anything more of Mickey, they should call. Becker's car was parked next to Buck's so he said he would follow them back to Truedell's home and watch her for another night. Penny and I went to our car and got in. I looked at her and the dog and laughed. She asked what was the matter with me. I said I was just happy we got out alive with no injuries.

We drove back, talking about the dog show. Penny was plotting to enter Willy in the next show since she had seen how it worked. I said I was all for it, but she'd have to do the actual showing of our baby while I watched proudly from the sidelines. She called me wuss and said I couldn't share in the glory when Willy came out on top. I dropped Penny and Willy off at the house and asked her if she minded if I went to Truedell's house for the night, to serve and protect. She said I just wanted to go have a pajama party with Buck and Becker, then she smiled and said to go take care of business, that she would call Eric to visit with her. I grinned and said to have fun, then drove off to Truedell's house.

I called Buck to tell him I was coming over. Becker yelled from the background that I should bring some pop. I said I would, stopped at a party store and got a twelve pack of beer, diet Sprite for Buck and a twelve pack of Pepsi for Becker, along with various snacks and nacho chips. When I got to Truedell's house, I was met by the cop out front. He asked where his libation was. I laughed, gave him two of the Pepsis and said that was as close to alcohol as he was getting. I drove up to the door as Buck and Becker came out to collect the goodies. We went into the living room, and Mrs. Truedell greeted me, thanking me for being there. Benny was relaxing on a chair. He had had a hard day.

We all relaxed, enjoying our refreshments and talking to Mrs. Truedell about how she had felt in the competition today. She said it was a real high without using drugs or alcohol, the thrill of competition and being in the winner's circle. I looked over to Benny and thought about all the things Mrs. Truedell would be putting him through, just like a stage mother.

I asked aloud how Mickey knew Mrs. Truedell was going to be at the dog show. Mrs. Truedell offered an explanation.

"My housekeeper said some man called just after we left and asked for me. Margaret told him I was at the dog show. He asked where it was, and she told him. She didn't think about what she was doing, just thought it was one of my customers, since they do call here. I can't be mad at her." We accepted that and all sat around talking about the show.

Around 11 p.m. the outside cop came rushing in with his gun drawn. I saw the gun before he even spoke and knew there was trouble.

He said quietly, "There a whole lot of movement outside around the house. I saw shadows and heard some noise. I went to the back of the garage, and it's all around us. I called in a request for back-up."

Just as he said that a volley of gun fire came ripping through the windows of the living room on all sides. Buck grabbed Mrs. Truedell, pushing her to the floor, and then reached over and pulled Benny down with them, covering the two of them the best he could. He turned the coffee table on its side and pulled it to them as a shield. Becker, the cop, and I had our weapons out and ready, but the blasts from what I presumed were automatic weapons held us down. Mickey had brought an army.

Buck had once mentioned to me that Truedell had a panic room, and I yelled to him to take her there. He nodded and got Truedell and Benny on the move, out of the living room and up to Mrs. Truedell's bedroom where the panic room was. I hoped they got up there safely. We just held ground while the windows and walls were being blasted. I was behind a big stuffed easy chair facing the hallway door when I saw a shadow on the floor. I hissed at Becker and pointed just as a man in black jumped out. Before he could pull off a few rounds into the room, both Becker and I laid him down with our weapons.

The cop was on the floor by a window, and he was blasting away by reaching up and firing through the window. I doubted he would hit anyone that way, but it created a diversion. I crawled to the hallway, and Becker followed. We came around the corner, and Becker fired over my head at a person coming in from the kitchen. He brought the man down. I hoped the cook and the housekeeper were hiding under their beds. We went toward the kitchen, jumping the body of the gunman, and carefully went in just as gunfire blasted through the kitchen windows and the back door. I hated the fact that we couldn't see who we were up against, couldn't even get a round off at anyone outside.

As Becker and I laid low I heard sirens in the distance and remembered the cop saying he called it in. I looked at Becker and said, "Back-up is on the way."

We were both lying behind the kitchen island when I heard the back door open. I saw a reflection in the stainless steel stove of two men walking in slowly. I signaled to Becker, and he saw the image, too. Becker went right and I went left around the counter, firing at the two men. They went down fast, and Becker and I ran to the open door leading to the garage. We went in and looked out the side garage windows. I saw three men in the yard still shooting at the living room windows. Becker and I carefully slid open the windows and started firing at the men. Two went down. One hightailed it to the woods. I went to the big garage door and looked out at the front yard just as a half dozen cop cars came roaring in. They came to a halt and, after surveying the situation, came out ready to fight.

I went to the window that looked out on the back yard and saw three men running up to the building, dropping low to the ground against the brick of the garage. It was an ambush position if the cops came around the side. I told Becker, and we went to the garage back door and burst out firing at the men. I rolled across the ground as they returned fire and got behind a brick BBQ. I fired around the structure and saw Becker was on the ground at the garage door firing at the men. All three were taken out just as the cops came barreling around the corner. Becker held up his badge, and I held up my hands. They stopped, and one cop, a friend of Becker's, smiled and asked if we needed any help. Becker got up and said to search the yard to see if they could find Mickey. They knew who he was from an earlier briefing.

About fifteen minutes later, the cops all gathered and said they couldn't find Mickey. Becker swore a curse I'd never heard him say before. He was pissed.

*

Chapter Twenty-seven

The bodies were gathered, and the meat wagon was called. I looked around for Buck and Truedell and realized they were still in the panic room. I whacked Becker on the arm and said to follow me. We went inside and upstairs to the bedroom. Just as we got to the bedroom door, I saw him. Mickey. He had a gun on Buck and Truedell and was smiling at Becker and me. He said to drop our weapons and come all the way in. Becker and I put our guns on the floor and came over to the bed. Mrs. Truedell was seated on the edge of the bed with Buck on the other side of the bed in front of the opening to the panic room. They'd never made it inside.

"So, Mickey, your boys started a diversion so you could slip in here?" I asked.

"Yeah, I was just interested in getting the old lady to where I could tell her what I thought of her before I kill her. The damn cops at the stadium messed up my plans, but I figured I could grab her later. I gathered some of the boys from my old gang and got them all revved up for blowing the house to bits. I just waited, and then came through my old bedroom window. I knew the lock was broken, still hadn't been fixed all these years. Then I came up here and waited." He grinned evilly.

Mistress Murders

"You know there are a whole lot of cops downstairs. Do you think you'll get out of here if you fire that gun?" Becker asked.

Mickey smiled and said, "I did live in this house till I was 15. I know it better than they do. I know ways out of here. They'll never find me."

Mickey bent down to Truedell who had a look on her face as if she wanted to kill Mickey herself. Mickey spit in her face and said, "You bitch, you made my life hell. You never cared for me, just packed me off to boarding school, and when I tried to get tossed out so I didn't have to be there, you moved me to a different one. You treated my old man like crap, too. That's why he killed himself, just to get away from you."

Truedell screamed, "He did not kill himself. He had a heart attack!"

"Yeah, the one you gave him! I wanted you dead, so I hired someone to kill you, but they screwed up. I came back thinking you were dead but, surprise, I see you at the airport calling me a bastard! After I got away from there I decided I wanted to tell you what I thought of you before I blow your fucking head off, just so you'll go to hell knowing why!" Mickey brought his hand up and slapped Truedell hard across the face. She cried out in pain.

Benny was sitting quietly by the side of the bed not understanding what was going on, but when Mickey slapped Truedell, Benny knew his mistress was being attacked, and that was not acceptable. The dog lunged at Mickey, going for the throat.

168

Bob Moats

Mickey was shocked and brought his arm up to ward off the attacking animal, then brought his gun up and fired at Benny. This diversion gave Becker and me time to spin and grab our guns. Becker was faster and fired three times at Mickey. I paused, waiting to see if he hit him. Mickey spun around and went down, blood spurting from his neck and head.

We went to him. Becker checked for vitals, found none. Truedell screamed, and we turned to see her on the floor with Benny. He was bleeding. Buck jumped over the bed and checked Benny. He pulled out his cell phone and dialed a number. He asked for Sue and then quickly told her what happened. He said he'd be there then hung up and grabbed the blanket off the bed. He spread it out on the floor, doubled it over, placed Benny on it and folded the rest around him. Buck stood with the dog and told Truedell to follow. They went toward the stairs.

By now, the other cops were coming up, ready for a gunfight, but when they saw Buck with the dog, they cleared the stairs. Becker yelled to the men to come up and guard the room Mickey was in until the forensic people could investigate. Buck and Truedell ran to his car. He going to put Benny in the back of his car, but Becker was behind them and told Buck to put the dog in a cop car. He told the nearest officer to drive them to the vet's office, full flashers and sirens.

The car screamed out of the drive and down the road with sirens blaring. I looked at Becker and said this was one hell of a pajama party. He grinned, and I knew he would gloat about this to Trapper. Speaking of him, Trapper's car came flying into the drive and screeched to a stop. He bounced out saying the watch commander called

169

him about a big gun battle. Becker filled him in on the whole fiasco as Trapper watched me. I grinned and nodded at whatever Becker told him. He got a big smile on his face, slapped Becker on his back, and said, good work. Becker got his goofy smile again.

Mickey's body was carried out by the ME after CSI took their pictures and checked the crime scene. Becker made his official statements to Trapper, and I backed him up. He said he would talk to Buck and Truedell for further statements.

Trapper, Becker and I sat on lawn chairs in the yard watching the activity. I had gone in to the fridge, startling the cook and housekeeper who finally came out of their rooms, and took out a couple of beers. Back out in the yard, I offered one to Becker. He sat looking at the can for a minute and then said, what the hell.

After about an hour everyone was gone leaving Trapper, Becker and me still sitting in the yard. Trapper asked where his beer was. I said he was driving. He said, who'd stop him? I laughed and tossed him a beer. My cell phone rang. It was Buck.

"Hello, hero," I said into the phone. He laughed.

"The vet got the bullet out of Benny and bandaged him up. He's going to be all right, but she said he might have a limp." He got quiet and continued, "That may mean that Benny's dog show days are over. The vet said maybe with therapy he'd be good again."

I felt bad for Benny and asked how Truedell was taking it. Buck said, "She was crying all over the place and said she just wanted Benny to be alive. He's sedated, but he'll be up and around tomorrow. The vet said he should stay in the clinic overnight to be sure. I offered to stay with him and so did the vet. She and I will be watching over the patient for the night. Truedell will be coming back with the cop."

I grinned and said, "Buck, you and the lady vet alone with nothing but wild animals around, be careful." He grunted and hung up.

I passed on the news to my gang and said Truedell would be back shortly. We sat there till she arrived, and I said I would stay the night to keep her company. Becker agreed. Trapper said he had papers to file and left. Mrs. Truedell sat with us on the lawn chairs. I offered her a beer. She looked at it, then said, "Hell, yeah." Becker and I laughed.

After a while Mrs. Truedell got quiet. "I never tried to be a bad mother. I just didn't know how to do it. There's no damn manual for raising a troubled kid. The experts don't have it down for every case. He got worse even through all my efforts to get him to be good. I tried easy, and then I tried hard. Neither way worked." She got quiet again.

I said, "Don't take it to heart. He had it in him to be bad. A lot of people have it built in, same as mental problems." I knew about that having been close to someone who had mental problems. "Nothing you could have done would have helped. He had it in him to go to this extreme. I'm sorry to say, but he's better off now."

She was close enough to me to pat my hand and say thank you. She stood and said she was worn out from the long day and was going to bed. Becker and I said our good nights to her, and we sat in the yard, just sitting back and looking up at the sky.

Becker finally broke the quiet of the night. "Do you think I'd make a good detective?"

"Barry, what I saw you go through the last couple days, I think you'd make a great detective. And I'll kill you if you repeat this, but Trapper told me he was grooming you to take his job when he retires in two years."

Becker looked at me and said, "No shit?"

I looked at him and said, "No shit."

*

Chapter Twenty-eight

Sunday morning came early. Becker was sleeping on the couch, and I was in an easy chair. Mrs. Truedell flitted around the house cleaning up the mess made by the gun fight last night. She had called a cleaning company so there were a number of people running around with vacuums and brooms, then came the glass company measuring the windows for replacements. An insurance agent surveyed the damage and presented Mrs. Truedell an estimate for repairs. She accepted the estimate, and he went off to file his paper work. I wondered how much all this would cost for people working on a Sunday morning.

Becker and I were soon back in the yard on the lawn chairs watching the activities. I thought it looked like the movie "The Money Pit," with Tom Hanks, where all the construction people were tearing apart and re-building the house. Becker said he loved that movie.

I pulled out my phone around 8:30 and called Penny. She answered after about five rings and said I interrupted her and Eric. I told her all about our adventures, and she was concerned about Benny. I said if Buck and the lady vet paid attention to him and not to each other, he would be fine. She asked when I would be home, and I said shortly, as soon as I could pin down Mrs. Truedell and see if she was going to be all right. We did our kissy-kissy on the phone and hung up.

I told Becker it was time for us to go back to our lives. He agreed. I went to Mrs. Truedell and said that our arrangement for protection was over, she was safe now. She told me to follow her, and we went into her home office. She got out her checkbook and wrote a check for me. I took it without looking, folded it and thanked her. She came to me, gave me a hug, and thanked me. I said she'd be all right. Buck would bring Benny back to her when the vet said he was ready to go home, and that she should just hang in there and call me if she had any problems.

I went out to where Becker was standing by his car. I said I'd talk to him later. We got into our cars and he left. I took a moment to look at the check. Mrs. Truedell's bill would have been $300 a day for five days or $1,500 total.

173

Mistress Murders

The check was made out for $5,000. I knew she didn't make a mistake. A woman in her position didn't do such things. She had given us a bonus. I would split the check with Buck. We both earned it.

I got home, and Penny was not around. I called and heard a small yip coming from the kitchen. Willy was blocked in the kitchen. There was a note taped to the board across the kitchen door saying not to move this board, just to come into the bedroom. I smiled and went to the bedroom. I didn't come out for the next two hours.

We had something to eat. Willy was mad at us for leaving him alone so long. I thought about Mickey and told Penny we would have to be careful bringing up our child.

After we relaxed a bit with the baby, I went to my computer desk and took out the paper we got from the puzzle box. I wrote down the numbers and the pin code and sat looking at them.

"I wonder if David Paul has these numbers already," I mused.

"Well, there's only one way to find out. We go to the islands and check it out," she said happily, seeing a vacation in her future.

I smiled and said, "OK, we go south and check on it. Do you know a travel agency that would handle such a trip?"

"I know just the place. It's run by an old friend of mine, my college roommate."

Bob Moats

"I never knew you were in college. I'm crushed that we never talked about that part of your life," I said.

"I studied communications at Michigan State for all of eight months before I left to go to Macomb community college. My money was getting low." She flashed her cute little smile.

"So can you call your personal travel agent and get us down to the Cayman Islands without stowing away on a garbage scow?"

She said she would see if she could reach her old friend, and bounced off to make the call. I knew she was excited to go back to the islands, and I could use a vacation after going through a gun fight involving automatic weapons.

I decided to call Buck. He answered after about six rings. "Hey, Jimmy, you survived the fun last night?"

"I'm a little sore but alive. How's Benny doing?"

"He's awake, and I'm going to take him home shortly. I called Mrs. Truedell to let her know his prognosis for better health, and she's happy. I'll take him home when Sue says it's all right."

"Speaking of Sue, how did you two get along last night?" I grinned.

"Well, Jimmy, I wouldn't marry her, I'm not ready to do that, but I like her. We got along good. She love bikes and once had a Harley but her ex took it in the divorce. I'm feeling good about her."

175

Mistress Murders

Penny came bouncing back into the room and saw I was on my cell phone. She went to sit on the couch to wait, but I could see she was anxious to talk.

"I got paid by Truedell. I think you'll be happy with what she gave us. Stop by tomorrow and I'll give you your pay. Penny and I are going to take a little vacation and do some business in the Cayman Islands for a couple of days. Oh, and when we get back there's a little matter of a trip to a strip bar." He let out a little cheer and said he'd be ready for that.

We finished our conversation and I hung up, then looked at Penny who had a wide smile.

"I talked to Lynda, and she said she could get us on her agent's discount to Miami. It's a short jump from there to the Cayman Islands. She just needs to know when we'll be going."

"I'll let you know later today after I do some checking about the progress of Richmond's investigation and the whereabouts of David Paul. He may have already got to the funds and vanished." She looked sad, so I continued. "But we'll go even if there's no money to find. I haven't had a vacation in years, and I'd love to be in paradise with you." That brought her smile back. I also said we'd have to do something with Willy. She had forgotten about that. I said I was sure Buck would watch him. He had Yorkies in the past. Penny said that would work for her, and she would get Willy's things ready for him. Then she said she was going to pack and toddled off to the bedroom.

It was Sunday and I wasn't sure if Richmond would be in his office. Did detectives take weekends off? I called, and he answered sounding sleepy.

"Are you awake?" I asked.

"Who the hell is this?" he grumbled. I told him. "Well, your suspect Paul has vanished, and I think he may have beat feet for the Caymans."

"I guess he must have the account numbers or he would be hanging around here to cover his ass. Now he doesn't care what you guys think when he may have millions at his fingertips. My girlfriend and I are going down there to take a little vacation and see if there's anything to Mr. Paul's disappearance. Are you any closer to getting the facts straight on the murder?"

"Well, we did find a wino who hangs around that motel to dumpster dive. He said he saw a person covered in blood and looking like Paul sneak out to a car matching Paul's Cadillac. The wino was afraid when he saw the blood and ran off. He came back last night to hit the dumpster again, and one of my men was there, so he nabbed him. I think Paul set up the farce and made it look the way it did to draw us off him. The wino said he didn't look drunk. He just sneaked to the car and got in with a key. We were lied to."

"Well, I presume you have a warrant out for him?"

"Bet your ass we do. I want that fucker back here so we can run him through the gauntlet. We've got all the airports on alert for him, but there are too many ways he can slip out. He could drive down to Florida and take a puddle jumper out to the islands. I'm calling the police down there this afternoon and faxing his photo to them. If you find anything let me know."

"I will. I'll talk later." We hung up, and I sat back thinking. Paul probably would take a car as far south as he could and go to the islands from that point, which meant I might still get there before him. I called Buck again and told him that Penny and I might head south sooner, so I would give him a check for his pay if he would swing by the house shortly. He said he would come over immediately, before he took Benny back to Truedell's. I asked if he could do us a favor and take Willy while we were gone. He said he'd love to, that he still had a few toys from his Yorkies that Willy could play with. I said that would work. We hung up, and I went to my desk to write out a check for Buck and call Penny. She came out, and I told her to call her agent friend back. I said we were going today, as soon as she could get us on a plane. Her eyes went wide, and she ran for the phone.

*

Chapter Twenty-nine

Penny was bouncing off the walls and called Lynda to set up the flight. She took care of the arrangements and then hung up.

"We can be on our way by 4:30, and Lynda will get hotel reservations for us at the same hotel I stayed at last time I was there. It's a great place as you saw in the video."

I said perfect and went to pack a bag. Buck came by about a half hour later, and I handed him the check. His eyes bugged out when he saw the amount. I told him Truedell gave us a bonus, so enjoy it. He said he would, shook my hand and said to be careful on our trip. Penny had Willy all packed up to go to Buck's house, she said her tearful goodbye to the dog, and they left. Penny and I finished getting our stuff together. I couldn't figure how Penny could pack four suitcases so fast. I said we were only going to be there a couple of days. She said she had to be ready for anything.

Lynda called back with instructions for picking up our flight tickets and where to meet the plane that would take us to Miami. When we got there, we'd have to get a connecting flight to the Caymans. We threw everything in the car, drove over to the freeway and down to Metro Airport, my second time in the last few days. We got to the counter and checked in. They sent the bags off into the bowels of the airport. I hoped they made it to the islands with us. We had to suffer through the search line. I hated removing my shoes. I also hated to leave my Glock back

179

at the house but I was pretty sure the gun would be something they wouldn't want traveling on their planes.

Then came the big wait till time to board the plane. We were sitting there when as a man came up and asked if I was Jim Richards. I said yes. He identified himself as an officer of the Madison Heights police. He said he was sure it was me since he saw me with Detective Richmond earlier in the week. He was assigned to the airport to be available if Paul came through. I wished him luck as I wanted him caught as much as Richmond did.

Finally they called for boarding on our plane. We went on by seating numbers. Penny and I made our way onto the crowded plane and found our seats. I liked the corporate jet we took to Vegas better, more leg room. Lynda was only able to get us in coach for her discount, but we didn't complain. I thought that with all the money between Penny and me we could have gotten first class. The trip back would be different even if I had to exchange the tickets. We also had the pleasure of an obese man sitting at the window on our seat row who, after the plane departed, decided to go the restroom every 15 minutes causing Penny and me to have to get up and down.

Penny looked at me and said, "There's going to be a hurricane sweeping the islands. I can tell from our trip so far."

I laughed and watched the people on the plane who looked uncomfortable with Penny's forecast. The flight attendants came around asking if we wanted nuts or pretzels. I imagined the first class passengers dining on shrimp and beer. I looked at Penny and said I was going to kill Lynda if we survived the flight. Three hours later the pilot came on and said we'd be arriving in Miami in about a half hour but might have to circle for a while till the storm there passed. Penny grumbled, "I knew it."

The plane finally touched down and after a half hour wait, it was moved to the unloading position. We went out the ramp door, and I felt like kissing the ground. We still had to rush across the airport to find our plane to the islands. I asked at an information counter, and the frazzled looking woman gave us directions to the tiny airlines that flew in and out of the Cayman and Jamaican islands. I thought since we would have to avoid Cuba I hoped it wasn't too tiny of an airline. We arrived at the Island Air counter, gave our names and were told that the plane would be boarding in a half hour. Penny and I looked out the window at the cloudy gray skies over Miami. Penny was still grumbling about our luck, and I turned her to me and gave her a hug and a kiss.

"Any place I'm with you is sunny and warm. Let's just make the best of it."

She kissed me on the nose and said, "Bite me." I laughed, and then she did, too.

The woman at the boarding counter announced that they would start taking on passengers. We got in line. This one wasn't as formal as the major airlines, and there were fewer people getting on. We were brought on and seated then told what to do in a water crash, which made me nervous as I didn't like being in water. The plane taxied out and went up into the dark clouds. We finally broke above them into a brilliant blue sky. Penny had the window seat and felt a little better now that she could see the sun just as it was setting below the horizon.

Mistress Murders

After we missed Cuba, the pilot announced the plane was heading into Owen Roberts International Airport, Georgetown, Grand Cayman. He hoped we enjoyed our flight and our stay on the island.

I had the address of the Deutsche Bank Limited branch in Georgetown, and I wanted to be there in the morning first thing. It was almost 10 p.m., and we were worn out from the trip down. We deserved a vacation from that alone. A half hour later the plane landed safely. We left the airport and found the guest bus for the Ritz Carlton Hotel. The bus was air-conditioned, a good thing since the night air was hot and muggy. We arrived at the hotel, our bags were taken by a porter, and we went to the desk to sign in. At least they had our reservations. We were escorted to our room which had a beautiful view of all the lights of the city. Penny crashed on the bed and said not to disturb her till morning. I asked if she was hungry. She popped back up and said she was hoping I wouldn't mention it. She was, so we changed from the clothes that had been with us for a couple thousand miles, and Penny led me to the restaurant she liked from her previous visit.

We had arrived on the island too late to see the sunset on the beautiful Seven Mile Beach, so we just explored the city. The night life was lively, and Penny took me to some of her past haunts. We had cocktails and beer in a quiet café and then went outside where Penny hailed a cab. She told the cabbie to go to the clock tower at Edwards and Fort Street. We got out, wandered around looking at the sites, and found a small bar with live musicians playing local music.

Bob Moats

Shortly after midnight we caught another cab and went back to the hotel. We crashed into bed and barely made out before both falling asleep. I woke around 4 a.m. and went to the balcony looking out over the hotel pool at the huge Caribbean Ocean. It was too dark to see the blue-green waters that I had studied from my computer at home, but I could imagine them. I turned and looked at the beautiful woman in the bed, sleeping so peacefully. How could I not love her? I came back to bed and cuddled with her then drifted back to sleep.

The next morning, we arose and I again looked out at the water, now a brilliant blue-green. All around tourists were sun bathing and swimming in the pool. We dressed and went down to find a place to get a light breakfast, but not in the hotel, some place native. We walked around the nearby streets, found a small diner, and went in to eat. I tried my cell phone, but it had no reception there. I'd leave it in the room next time, but I knew I would feel naked without it.

We finished our meal. I signaled for a cab and asked him to take us to the nearest police station. He asked if we were robbed. I said no, we just had some police business. He smiled and took us to the headquarters of the Georgetown police. We went in and were greeted by a huge man in a khaki uniform sitting at a small desk in the large hallway. I showed him my P.I. license and explained that I was hunting for a fugitive from Michigan in the states and wondered if I could talk to an official. He smiled, made a call and shortly a man came out and directed us to an office where a smaller man sat at a very ornate desk. He stood and introduced himself as Captain Barrows-White of her Majesty's Cayman Island Police. I knew the islands were under British sovereignty, but I thought there would be plain old local police. Didn't matter. I explained that I was hunting a man who might have come to the island and Georgetown. I took out a picture of Paul to show him.

He smiled, said he had already seen the picture, that it had been sent by email to him from the FBI in the States with a request that he be looking for the man. He had it circulated to his men. I was surprised that the request came from the FBI, but it was a bank being robbed, FBI jurisdiction, and Richmond probably was palming it off on them. Plus we had crossed international lines so having the feds in on it made it more legal. The Captain mentioned Richmond's name, and I said I was working the case with him. He said that the FBI said to get in touch with him if the suspect showed up. He asked where we were staying, and I told him. He said he would keep me informed if Paul showed up. I told him we were going to the bank that Paul was suspected of having dealings with. I was being deliberately vague about the embezzlement and the fact we had the account numbers. I thanked him and we left.

Penny was impressed with the cooperation of the local police and the reach that the feds had. I said I hoped they found him.

*

Chapter Thirty

We left the police station and hailed a cab, asking to be taken to the Deutsche Bank Limited. I gave him the address. He dropped us off at the front of the bank. We went to the doors where we met two guards just inside the entrance. They stopped us and asked what our business was. We told them we wanted to get into an account. They asked for ID, and we showed them our passports. I thought this was a bit more security than found in the U.S. Maybe if our banks had something like this there would be fewer robberies.

We went up to a desk and asked the girl seated there where we could get into and check on an account. The girl led us to a man at a desk off to the side of the room. He stood and introduced himself as Klaus Deiter. He asked us to sit, and I said I needed to check on an account in his bank. He asked if we were the account holder. I took out my P.I. identification and showed it to him. I hoped he wasn't aware of exactly what that entailed and would think it was some kind of law enforcement agency in the States. I was right. He asked how he could help the American police. I explained the embezzlement attempt made from the Bank of America and how the funds were transferred to his bank. He said quietly that a number of American businesses and persons had accounts there that the United States IRS would love to know about. He grinned.

I asked if we could access the account. He wanted to know if we had the account number and pin code. I took out the paper and read the numbers to him as he typed into the computer. He asked the name on the account, and I took a stab and said Marsha Webster. He smiled, put a keypad in front of me and asked if I would enter the pin code. I just sat looking at the keypad. It contained only numbers, no letters. I looked at Penny and held up the paper with the letters AEIOS written on it.

Penny got a look on her face like she was thinking hard and then said, "OK, Mr. computer whiz, when you told me how to hide a password for entering a secure site, what did you tell me about number-letter substitutions?"

I looked at her, then at the paper, and suddenly it dawned on me. I smiled and said she was handy to have around. She asked if she was finally on the payroll. I said we'd discuss it later. In the past I had told Penny that a good password would have both letters and numbers, but that made it hard to remember. So I told her if she took a word like Richards, she could just type in the password, "richards" but that would be too easy. If she used number-letter substitution the name would be r-1-c-h-4-r-6-5. Using: 1=i, 2=S, 3=E, 4=A, 5=S, 6=b or d, 7=T, 8=B and 9=g. An easy memory aid.

I looked at the AEIOS and deduced it to be 4-3-1-0-5. I typed it into the keypad. Mr. Deiter smiled and said it worked. I asked for a print out of the balance. He hit a few keys and gave me the paper that came out of the laser printer. I looked at it and about had a stroke. One point three million dollars. I showed it to Penny. She just said wow.

I asked Mr. Deiter if I would be able to change the pin number to prevent the fugitive from accessing the account, and he said, of course. He typed something on his computer, then told me to enter the pin number again on the keypad. I did and then he said to enter the new pin and hit enter then do it again. When I finished, he smiled and said the criminal would no longer be able to access the account. I gave him a picture of Paul, said to watch for him, and told him where we could be reached, though he should call Captain Barrows-White at police headquarters first. I said the local police were on the lookout for him. He grinned and said he loved watching "Law and Order" on their local cable TV, that it was so realistic. I thanked him and said we would be in touch with the U.S. bank fraud and security about transferring the money back to Bank of America. He said he enjoyed our visit and please come back anytime. We left with the door guards smiling at us.

I told Penny when I was in Germany during my Army stay there, I found the Germans to be very open and friendly. They smiled a lot. She said it was probably from all the beer. I agreed.

As we walked around the streets of Georgetown taking in the sites, I smiled at the fact that I had the only pin number that would take someone to one point three million dollars. If I wasn't an honest man, I would have made off with the money myself, but I didn't want to be a fugitive. In real life the fugitives usually get caught. We took a cab back to the hotel where Penny slapped on her bikini and wanted to go down and sunbathe. I wasn't one to do such a silly thing, so I just went with her and sat reading a new e-book by Robert B. Parker on my Palm TX, a Spenser book I hadn't read yet. We were relaxing by the pool when a porter came up and asked if I was Jim Richards. I said I was, and he said there was a call for me from the States. He told me where to take it, and I went to the phone and answered. The operator connected me. It was Richmond.

"How's the sunny paradise going?" he asked.

I laughed and said it was great, no storms and I was now the only person that had access to the embezzled money. He asked if Paul was anywhere around. I said he hadn't popped up, and I was surprised that Richmond's name had been thrown around by the local police. He said by bringing in the FBI, it was easier to get cooperation with the British cops. I said it worked for me. I told him we would be coming back on Wednesday morning, and I hoped I didn't run into Paul till after then because I wanted to enjoy my time in the sun. He laughed and said he'd see me later then hung up.

I turned to see if Penny was still enjoying her sunbathing, but she wasn't there. I went to her towel and looked around for her. I didn't see her anywhere. I figured she'd just gone to the ladies' room, and I turned to go there when I came face to face with Linda Shank.

I was startled, to say the least. She stood in front of me and asked what was the pin number. I said, "I'm sorry, but what do you mean?"

"Don't fuck with me. We know you changed the pin number. What is it, or we'll kill your lovely Penny."

My blood froze. I moved closer to her and asked what she had done with Penny. She said Penny would be released if I just gave her the pin number to the bank account. I asked where David Paul was. She said probably floating down the Detroit River by now. I looked at her and was wondering what she was talking about when Rene Paul came up behind her. Now I was really shocked. Rene said she was sorry for not sending me a check for watching David, but she was a little short on funds. She said she hired me to establish his involvement in the murder, but now I had screwed up their plans to get the money out of the account. "Nice work, Mr. Richards," she said.

I said if they hurt Penny, I would die before I gave them the pin. They said Penny probably would die first, would I like that? Linda pushed a small caliber gun in my ribs and told me to move towards the gate out of the pool area. I started that way, knowing I couldn't do anything till I saw Penny was all right. Linda and Rene led me to the parking lot and over to a white van with some cable TV company logo on the side. Rene knocked on the side door. It opened. Penny was sitting inside on the floor with the man Rene said was her lawyer the day I interrupted them at her home kneeling next to her with a knife in his hand.

I stood my ground and demanded to know what this was about. Rene came forward with a smile on her face, wanting to gloat about her almost perfect plan.

"Linda came to me one day and told me about David's involvement in Marsha's embezzlement. I found out from Linda that David was planning to get the account numbers from Marsha and then kill her, taking all the money. Linda and I became good friends years back when David was cheating on her with me. We plotted this all out when he told Linda about his intentions, and I involved you as a cover for our story. But you didn't cooperate by staying around at the motel or you would have seen Donald here pretending to carry David out to establish his innocence.

189

Since we saw you left early, I changed our plans and had Linda call David on his cell and tell David to go with his plan. He murdered Marsha then went to his car and took a sedative to confuse the cops. Everything went according to plan. Later Linda and I would set it up so David would finally be blamed for the murder and taking the money out of the account. The cops would think he got away, and Linda and I would get away with all the cash. We killed David and dumped him in the lake off his precious boat just before we took it down the river to Toledo where we had a car waiting to drive to Miami then to the islands and into the bank. But you had to screw things up again by coming here and messing with the account. Rene and I went into the bank, and I pretended to be Marsha, but the bank man said you had been there and changed the pin."

Linda said, "Mr. Richards, please give us the pin or we will have to do something harsh to your lady friend."

*

Chapter Thirty-one

"Gee, Linda, I thought you were a good person. That's why I didn't turn you into the cops the day you came to my office with the gun." I looked into the van. There was a pile of pipes on the floor next to Penny. I said to Penny that this reminded me of her abduction in Vegas. Rene told me to shut up and give out the pin. I hoped Penny would see my eyes looking in the direction of the pipes. She did.

Linda had the small gun on me, and the man had a knife at Penny. She slowly reached down towards the pipes and then yelled loudly, "Son of a bitch," while grabbing one and swinging the pipe up to hit the man squarely in the head. Linda looked startled, momentarily turning the gun towards Penny and giving me time to grab her hand. I twisted the gun from it just as she fired the tiny weapon. I managed to get it away from her as Rene ran from the scene. I pushed Linda down into the van and held the gun on both her and the man. Penny jumped out and stood next to me. I said for Penny to go get a cop or someone. She ran off, but didn't have to go far. A cop nearby had heard the gun fire and was heading in our direction. Penny got his attention, and he came over to us. I explained to him what had happened and that Captain Barrows-White would back up our story.

Penny and I sat in police headquarters for about an hour while the Captain sorted everything out. He came to us, said he had talked to Detective Richmond, and they were arranging for extradition of Linda and Donald back to the states. I thanked him and asked if they had any word on Rene Paul. He said no, but she wouldn't be able to get off the island without them catching her unless she swam back to the states. He laughed at his joke and then said he'd keep me informed as to the progress. I thanked him, and Penny and I went back to our hotel where we changed clothes and went to dinner at the nicest restaurant we could find. Later we celebrated in bed. We spent another day exploring the island and its historical sites then arranged for our return the following morning. I made sure we were going first class all the way.

The next morning we flew from the islands and landed in Miami then over to Delta for our flight to Metro

Mistress Murders

Airport. I tried my cell phone and got reception. I called Buck to tell him we were on our way home and would see him later. They called for our flight to board, and we entered the plane. The first class was great, plenty of legroom. When the flight attendant asked what we'd like to drink, I smiled and asked if they had beer. She said they did. I asked how long we had till we got into Metro. She checked her watch and said about three hours. I said, bring me two beers, and she went off. Penny said I better not get drunk. I said I was getting one for her so we could get drunk together. She smiled and said thank you. I leaned back and relaxed. This was the way to travel.

We got into Metro Airport about 1 p.m., managed to find all our baggage off the carousel, and dragged it to our car. We paid the ransom to get the car out of the parking structure, and we were finally back on I-94 heading home.

I told Penny I enjoyed the vacation, but it was good to be back. She had to agree, saying she hadn't planned on spending her time in paradise sitting in the back of a dirty van. I smiled, and reached over and took her hand. We got back to the house by 2:30, and I called Buck to return our child. He said he'd be right over and hung up.

Buck pulled in and Willy went crazy, jumping all over us and wagging his stub of a tail. I asked if Buck had spent all his money yet. He said he bought a few new parts for his cars but still had enough to enjoy life. He went off, and I told Penny we had a little business to take care of and we could bring the puppy with us. She got the doggy purse. I put him in, and we went out to Penny's car.

I drove over to the headquarters of Bank of America and into Sitaro's office. I had called earlier to be sure he was in and his secretary had set a time for me. Sitaro came out and led Penny and me to his office. We sat. He smiled and asked what he could do for us.

"I think it's what I can do for you. When I was last here you said there was a finder's fee if I could return the embezzled money from Marsha Webster." He nodded. "Well, I have your money in an account in the Cayman Islands." I paused for effect then continued, "I have the only pin code to access that account. If you'd like your money back, I'd like a cashier's check for its return."

He got a big smile on his face and asked how much were we talking about. I gave him the printout from the German bank. His eyes went wide, and he whistled low.

"Well, my computer people said it would be substantial. I see they were right. If you'll excuse me for a moment, I need to talk to our senior bank officer." He got up and went out. Penny and I sat quietly. Willy just snorted and put his head down on Penny's arm. We started talking about our vacation, and I said our next would be back to Vegas. She agreed.

After about a half hour of waiting, Sitaro came back to his desk with a check in his hand. He held it out, but when I stretched to reach for it, he pulled back and asked for the bank information. I smiled, took out the paper I had the account number on, picked up a pen from his desk and added the pin code. I handed it to him. He studied it, then handed me the check.

"Any word on David Paul?" he asked.

Mistress Murders

"David Paul is sleeping with the fishes," I said. "He was murdered, also over the money. I'm glad to get it back to you."

"Sorry to hear of his death, but justice is served." We stood. I thanked him, he thanked me, and then Penny, Willy and I went back to our car.

I sat and looked at the check, let out a loud whistle and showed it to Penny. Her mouth fell open when she saw the amount, $130,000. I said it was ten percent, standard finder's fee. She grinned and said we were going to Vegas on the first flight out. I said I had some things to take care of first.

We went back home after I stopped at the bank to deposit the check. I went to my desk, got out my check book and wrote a few checks, then put them in envelopes and wrote names on them. When I walked out to the kitchen, Penny was making a late lunch of sandwiches and soup. We were eating when my cell phone rang. It was Richmond.

"Richards, first, thanks for making my life easier. To sum up the case, we got Linda Shank and the man back to the states, and they're on their way up here. FBI is helping me with it. I got a few friends in the bureau. David Paul's body was pulled out of the Detroit River this morning by Detroit Harbor cops. He did have ID on him so it made it easier to track him down from the warrant. Rene Paul was apprehended in Jamaica. She took a boat over to the island, and the Kingston police nabbed her in town. We're working on getting her back. I'm sure we can convince Linda to spill all the details of the crime. If not, I'd like your take on it."

"I'd be glad to come in and talk. Just let me know." We finished and hung up.

I related to Penny what Richmond told me and then called Trapper. He came on and said it'd been peaceful for the last couple of days without me around. I laughed and told him the story of our adventures. When I got to the finder's fee check, he just said wow and asked for a loan. I laughed and said, no chance. I asked him how Becker was doing, and Trapper said he was gloating all over the place. Trapper had to send him out on road patrol so he'd remember what it was like.

I said I had some errands to run and would be in contact later. I made another call and asked Ben Webster if he was around Ballywick. He said he and his sister were taking a little time to themselves to remember Marsha. I said I had to stop by to drop something off. He said he'd wait for me. I gathered up Penny and the pooch, and we drove over to Helen Webster's home. Ben came out to greet us. I handed him an envelope and explained that it was part of the money from the return of the embezzled funds. I was giving it to help with Marsha's burial. He said he didn't want any part of stolen money. I explained it wasn't stolen, it was the reward for returning the stolen money. Besides, with the puzzle box, he helped find it, so part of the reward was his. He smiled and introduced his sister when she came out of the house. We talked for a bit, then I said I had other places to go. We said good-bye and good luck and left. He and his sister stood as he opened the envelope. I turned back to see him looking at me with a startled expression, holding the check for $50,000 so his sister could see it, too.

Mistress Murders

As we drove back home, Penny said that was a nice thing I did for them. She leaned over and kissed me on the cheek.

Later in the evening, I made a few calls to people inviting them to the house. After everyone arrived, Penny and I sat in the backyard with Buck, Trapper and Becker. I gave them each an envelope and said it was thanks for helping with the two cases we just closed. I told them not to open the envelopes until they were home. Then I gave an envelope to Penny. She smiled and asked if this was her payroll finally. I bent down and kissed her and said, you bet. They all sat back and relaxed with beer and pop as I cooked some big juicy steaks on the grill.

It was good being with friends.

The End.

For every ending, there's a new beginning...

*****

Bob Moats

preview of the next Jim Richards book,
"Bridezilla Murders"

Prologue

I hated phone calls in the middle of the night; they either woke me rudely or were bad news. The call at 4 A.M. was bad news.

I rolled over and grabbed the phone, hopefully before it woke Penny, although she could sleep through a nuclear attack. I almost rolled over Willy, our toy Yorkie, sleeping soundly next to me; he yelped and ran to the foot of the bed. I got to the phone just before its third ring and said hello. It was my brother; I just knew what he was going to tell me, our father had passed away.

Before I moved in with Penny, I had lived with my parents, helping my Mother with my Dad who was a stroke victim. His health went downhill over the years since that first stroke, and he wasn't getting any better after I moved out. I knew it was going to happen one day, but that didn't make it any easier. I hated to see him just sitting in his room watching crappy TV, which was all he seemed to want. I would stop by a couple times a week and he was not well, I could tell.

Penny was lying next to me listening to the fragments of my conversation with my brother and after I hung up and laid back, she pulled me to her. I laid there for what seemed like days.

We were dressed early and on the way to the cemetery two days later, my Mom not wanting a funeral, just family and very close friends at the burial. I refused to view my

197

father in the coffin; I wanted to remember him alive, not laid out all made up like a mannequin. Dad was put in the crypt with military honors, a 21 gun salute and they gave the flag to Mom. We all ended up at a local restaurant for breakfast and then parted to go on with our lives.

I was driving back from the restaurant and I would glance over to Penny when I could. She was so beautiful to me and I loved her. I was feeling a bit mortal now; I'm 60 years old and I would never know when I would go out of life as well. We got back to the house and I took Penny to the living room and sat her down on the couch. I paused a bit too long and she asked if I was all right.

"I'm sad, but what I want to say is something I have thought about for a long time." I paused again; she waited. "We've been together for almost a year now and I love loving you. You amaze me every day with your silly little skits and shows, I am always wondering what to expect when I get home. I don't want to lose that."

I got down before her on the couch and said, "I'd be honored if you would be my wife, my love and my life."

Penny's eyes went wide and she got a strange look on her face, happy yet stunned. She took my face in her hands and kissed me fully and firmly. She pulled back and said, "What took you so long?" I laughed and she continued, "I have never met a man quite like you, smart, funny and a passion for life. Yes, I would want to be your wife and have you as my love and my life." She kissed me again.

Bob Moats

Chapter 1

I stood and pulled her up and told her to grab Willy's carrier and she did. I put Willy in the doggy purse that I had Penny wear, and aimed her for the door. She asked where we were going, I said you'll see. We got in the car and I drove over to the Macomb Mall and into Zale's Jewelers. She smiled and said she wanted the biggest rock they had; I said it would be a nice rock. The salesgirl went nuts over Willy, then showed us different engagement and wedding rings, we took our time, just to get it right.

I still had a huge nest egg from the check I got for the finder's fee from Marsha's embezzlement during the mistress murders, so I didn't care how much the rings cost. We picked out a very nice set and luckily they had them in our sizes. I paid the cashier and we went out.

Penny asked me on the way to our house if we should have a nice quiet wedding, just friends and family or an elopement to Las Vegas. I laughed and thought about it, Vegas would be nice, and we'd be able to see Deacon and Lynn. I looked at her and asked if she wanted to do that. She said the logistics would be difficult, bringing my mother and family all the way out there, not to mention Buck and Trapper if they wanted to go, but she really would like the idea. We got back to the house and sat talking about how we could pull it off. I got on the phone and called Vegas and got Lynn. It was about 9 A.M. in Vegas and Lynn sounded like she just got up.

"No work today for the wicked," I asked after putting them on our speaker phone. She recognized my voice, shrieked and called Deacon. I heard him grumbling about being woke so early. I said to Lynn to tell him to get the hell out of bed. Lynn told him who it was and he bellowed that it was about time I called.

After they both settled down and put me on their speaker phone, I said, "OK, here's the deal, Penny and I have decide to get married and we want to do it in Vegas." I waited for them to respond. They did with yelling and screaming, mostly Deacon was screaming.

Lynn said she had connections with some great wedding planners in Vegas and they would make it an affair to remember. That kind of scared me, but I saw Penny eyes light up.

"We're still in the planning stages, but we'll let you both know when we'll attempt it. We have to make sure everyone here can get time off to go, and if we can get them to agree to go out there."

We talked a bit more about life and I told them about my father, they gave their condolences. We said we'd be in touch soon and said our good-byes and hung up.

Penny had this look on her face that worried me; she looked devious. I asked what was on her evil mind. She said she had an idea to get everyone out to Vegas without having to suffer the airports of hell. I was intrigued, but she said I may not like the idea. I asked her to tell me, and I'd let her know if it was a good idea. She told me to wait and went to the phone in the bedroom, out of my hearing range. I was worried.

She was gone for about a half hour as Willy and I sat on the couch waiting. She came bouncing back into the room and said she made a deal with her producer, oh, and he said congratulations, that if the station can film the wedding for the show, they would send everyone out on the corporate jet we flew out the last time we were in Vegas. I sat looking at her thinking about the circus that this could become, but liked the idea of flying everyone out together for free, and avoiding, as Penny said, the airports of hell. The next thing we would have to attempt is to get everyone to agree on when they were free to go.

I knew my mother had all the time in the world now, but getting her to leave her home and board a plane may be a bit hard to get her to do. My brother was self-employed so he could adjust his life, I hoped. I wanted my son there, but he lived up north, about 250 miles away, I'd see if he could bring his wife and baby down to go with us. This could be a nightmare.

I called Buck and told him our plans and he whooped and hollered and asked when we were leaving. I said as soon as I get everyone to settle on dates and times. He said the second check I gave him for guarding Mrs. Truedell and her dog allowed him to have a lot of free time. I said I'd keep him informed.

I called Trapper, I wanted him to come with us, he was good people and he might get a kick going back to his home town of Las Vegas.

"Why do you want to spoil a good thing by getting married, Richards." Trapper said over the phone when I told him the plan.

Mistress Murders

"I've wanted to marry Penny for a long time, the events of the last week made me realize life can be short."

"Hey, I'm sorry to hear about your Dad. I'll have to see how much vacation time I have, of course the check you gave me allows for any unpaid time off I'd want, but I may be able to swing it, as soon as you let me know when we can go. I think I'd like to go back to my roots, and especially to go harass my old buddy, Captain Weber." I could see him smiling wide through the phone. We finished up and he hung up.

I looked to Penny and said that today was not a good day to talk to my Mom, so soon after the burial, so we'd wait a couple of days and hit her with it. I called my brother and told him, he congratulated us and said it sounded good, if the trip was free. I said it would be if we can get everyone together. He said to let him know.

I was feeling like this was not going to be easy. I called my son up in northern Michigan and told him, he said he and his family would love to come. He was unemployed, but I sent a check from my windfall to help them out, and they were free to go. I said they would have to drive down when we decided to go.

Penny and I sat and drew out a plan on paper and finally came up with an approximate date to make it all happen, it mostly depended on my Mom. Penny called her producer and he said he'd arrange for the jet and the film crew when we had a definite date. The film crew idea still scared me.

We sat back on the couch and soaked in the moment. Penny was admiring her big rock, commenting on how we'd be Mr. and Mrs. soon. She would have to keep her last name due to her show, but she would hyphenate it off the show. Willy was having fits that we were ignoring him; Penny picked him up and rubbed his belly, he forgave us.

The next morning we were up early and dressed. Earlier in the week, Penny had told her producer about the funeral and told them she was taking a couple days off. The station would run repeats till she was able to return. We had breakfast, I usually don't, but I was hungry this morning. I guess it had to do with all the pre-marital celebrating we did in bed last night.

I called my Mom and said we'd like to stop by, she said she'd like that. We packed up Willy and headed off see if we could get Mom to leave her home, get on an airplane that she's never been on before and fly two thousand miles to watch us tie the knot. Mission Impossible.

We got there and she showered Willy and Penny with hugs and kisses and told us to come and sit. We did and Mom told us how she started cleaning the house and packing away Dad's stuff. She pulled out a small box and gave me a choice of my dad's rings and I picked a nice silver one, my brother would get the other gold one.

She said we looked like we had something on our minds. We hesitated not knowing how she'd take it so soon after the funeral.

"Mom, I realized yesterday that life was precious and I wanted to make Penny an honest woman, so I asked her to marry me and she accepted." I waited.

Mom went crazy happy and jumped up to hug and kiss Penny, then me. I hated getting sloppy with that kind of happy, but it made Mom feel good. She asked when and I hesitated again.

"Well, that depends on you. We decided to get married in Las Vegas, and Penny arranged for her station to fly all of us out in the corporate jet to Vegas for free, and avoiding commercial airline headaches. I talked to my brother and my son and they are all for it, we just need to know if you are agreeable to going with us." I paused waiting for the reasons for her not going so far away.

She surprised me by asking when was the flight out. I told her we still had to arrange it but it would be soon, in a week or so. She said she wouldn't miss it. I looked at Penny and said we had a go for everyone, now to herd them all into the plane.

Continued in the book

Bob Moats

Jim Richards Family of Readers

Thanks to the following people who are now part of the Jim Richards Family of Readers. They have read a book or more and enjoyed them. They all volunteered to be included in the list. If you are a fan of the books, send me your full name and you will be included in future books. Send your name to murdernovels@bobmoats.com to be added here and on the website. (updated 03-23-14)

* Achim Feifel * Al Norris * Alex Wheatley * Alexandra Delporte-Wilkinson * Amy Tapia * Andrea Bryan * Anne Shepherd * Arianda Sugar * Arlene Markowski * Ashley Augustus * Audra Hall * Barbara Hughes * Barbara Sammons * Barbara Schuler * Barbara Zirger * Beth Donohue Plenskofski * Betsy Childress * Beth Gibson * Bill Sandy * Bill Tornquist * Billie-jo Collie * Boni J Rychener * Carl Bishopric * Carla Lewis * Carole Henderson * Carolyn Conroy * Carolyn Riddle-Linington * Cassy Bailey * Chad Hudson * Charlotte L Duran * Cheryl L. Everett * Cindy Ackley Nunn * Cindy Valstad * Connie Bancroft * Corinne Kay O'Daniel * Dana Robbins Chuchran * Dana Wichita * Danielle Monique * Darren Heald * Dave Travers * David Wilkinson * DeAnn Jannereth * Deanna Miller * Deb Breuker Balbo * Debbie Carter * Debbie White * Deborah Fartuch * Deborah Gauze * Deborah Sullivan * Dee King * Denise Freeman * Diana Carver * Dixie Beck * Donna Gould * Donna Thompson * Donny Minter * Doris Kight * Eddie Moore * Eric Walters * Felicia Annette Bradfield * Francine Menor * Gail Chesney * Georgiann Minster * George Conner * Greg Colucci * Hayley Rankin * Harold

Mistress Murders

Garcia * Heidi Arnold * Irma Ranee Coy * Jacqueline Moss * Jan Kimball * Janice Schneider * Janice Spoor * Jennifer Redmond * Jessica Keown-Belous * Jim Beck * Jo Boguslaw * Jo Turner * Joanne Marie Turner * John Peiffer * John Wisbiski * Joseph Wauro * Joyce Stacy * Joyce Trifiletti * Judy Franklin * Judy Travers * Judy Padgett * Julie Heath * Junnahvee Benson * Karen Dahl * Karen Grams * Karen Higham * Karen Kaiser * Karen Meinburg Richwine * Karen Kirkman Parker * Karin Hawkins * Karin Vasvari * Kathleen Donohue Roesing * Kathleen Riddle-Wolfe * Kathy Hinds Moore * Kathy Jones * Kathy Mitchell * Katie Benzler * Kay Burns * Kelly Garcia * Ken Boggs * Keota Rodriguez * Kiera Mccarthy * Kim Estes * Kitty Stolle * Kristie Sciler * Kirsty Stanton * LaLonnie Scallen * Larry Morris * Leann Parr * Lenora Scales * Leslie Marie Jackson * Linda Forester * Linda Ingle Cox * Linda Kennerö * Linda Magill * Lisa Bower * Liz Gibson * Lorraine Wiman * Loretta Alexander * Lynda Bowles * Lynette Lawrance * LuAnn Louttit * Manny Rothman * Marcia Gibson DeWitt * Marie Calder * Marlene Bryan * MaryLouise Kramp * Mary Lynn Gross * Megan Atkins * Meghan Hyden * Melody Cannavan * Michael Carruthers * Michael Dinkens * Michael Vannoy * Michelle Burns-Mitchell * Michelle Pilcher * Micki Potter * Mike Moats * Mimi Baur * Myrna Hecht * Nadine Sutton * Natalie Quine * Neena Martin * O'Della Wilson * Pat Pollington * Pat Rohn * Patricia Jarmon * Patricia C Trezza * Patrick Barry * Paul Lawrance * Peggy Davis * Phyllis Bassett * Raylene Matheny * Rebecca Collins Besner * Renee Brumley * Reta Hanna * Reta Moats * Roberta Navarro-Harder * Sally Berneathy * Sally Hubler * Sarah Santos * Satka Nikc * Sharon E. Edwards * Sharon Mangini * Sharon McMillon * Sheena Rawl * Sherry Amstutz * Shirley Alvarez * Shirley Davies * Shirley Williams * Stacie Rowe * Stephanie Conner * Steve Cullen * Susan Haughton * Susan Hesse Adams * Susan Salomon * Suzan K Chase * Taisha Cullum

Bob Moats

Thank you to all these wonderful people.

Thank you for purchasing this book. I hope you enjoy it as much as I enjoyed writing it for my faithful readers. Please feel free to email me to tell me what you thought about my stories. I love hearing from the readers. I can be reached at murdernovels@bobmoats.com thanks again!